Dead End

Plight of Rudy Barabbas

Careful what you wish for—every choice brings consequence!

Novella 4

Yuan Jur

Cover art : Ralph Manis/Infinitee Designs

WAADOOM

Australia

Dead End by Yuan Jur

ISBN-13: 978-0-6481977-0-6 (Paperback)
ISBN-13: 978-0-6481977-3-7 (E-Book Epub)
ISBN-13: 978-0-6481977-2-0 (E-Book MOBI)

Cover and art design by Ralph Hawke Manis of Infinitee Designs © 2017
www.infinitee-designs.com
Book design and production by WaaDoom Press in association with Thebookpatch.com
Editing and structure by Charles Wannop and De Chao Peterson

Dedication

To the dedicated Citadel 7 crew. The guys and girls no one hears about.

The backers LMA, Editors JDK and Mary Rosenblum, Cover artist "Ralph the Brush Manis", production manager CW, Lauren—our admin wizard and beta testers NC, DW, Pearl & Co.

You all continue to be awesome! Thanks for helping the Citadel 7 fans Enter The Superverse ©, a domain created for all wanting to journey with their heroes in the Citadel 7 series, even when the journey may reveal more than they had intended to find.

Orders

"Welcome, Agent. This mission propels us along the Superverse Continuum through the endless oceans of Dark Matter. We will emerge in a timeline where some things will seem familiar, others quite strange. The voice of Central will now take you through our brief. See you on the ground. Mission success to us all!"

C-DATE: CLASSIFIED.
UNFOLDING TIMELINE: ACTIVE.
MISSION AUTHORIZATION: EVERCYCLE SEVEN.
MISSION POINT OF ORIGIN: MILKY WAY GALAXY, SOLAR SYSTEM, PLANET EARTH.
PLANET SECURITY LEVEL: 10.
LOCAL TIME/PLACE: 1978/UNITED STATES OF AMERICA.
CATALYST FOR EVENTS: DETECTION OF RIFT IN NATURAL KARMA STREAM HAS BEEN IDENTIFIED. IT IS THE DAY BEFORE COMMANDER BLOCH'S HISTORIC RETURN TO EARTH TO THWART THE VARIAN AND ECHAA INVASION OF THE SUPERVERSE M SYSTEM CORE.

ACT 1

CHAPTER

1

An Ordinary Man

The inside of the cab felt frigid in the midst of another bleak San Antonio winter. Rain dribbled down the smudged, foggy windows with depressing monotony. Outside, the dappled reflection of a nearby streetlight did little to lift the gloom. In the driver's seat shivered Rudy Barabbas, eager to finish the last forty-five minutes of his shift. Sunny Jamaica and all its tropical memories seemed a universe away now. His bad right knee hated this weather and throbbed in a grinding ache. He looked skyward through the top of the windshield, rubbing his gloved hands together.

"America ain't been no land of opportunity for old Rudy, then . . . has it, Goddess?"

On both sides of the bleak, low-rise street, some second-story windows presented shadows and silhouettes of occupants trying to keep warm behind drawn curtains. Rudy checked his watch again. Under the scratched face, hands pointed to 11:20.

"Come on, midnight."

Again he blew into his hands, trying to push away the persistent chill, and then he glanced at the item on the cab's bench seat beside him. His last fare had left behind a newspaper, which Rudy had retrieved from the backseat but not looked at since. Light through the passenger window highlighted the front page of that day's *San Antonio Express*. Rudy's eyes tracked downward from the

November 1978 date to the headline: *Keyhole Killer Murder No. 5*. A subhead read: *Police Seek Councilman Walter Kneebone as Possible Suspect.*

Rudy sighed and shook his head. *Goddess no, not another one.* He picked up the paper, his interest growing. At the beginning of the article was an unflattering picture of the prime suspect, which amounted to little more than a mug shot. The only thing missing was a jailbird number underneath.

Hoping to pass the time, Rudy skimmed over the entire article, shivering even more at the gruesome details of the latest murder by this so-called Keyhole Killer. When he'd finished reading the entire piece, he gazed at the larger photo toward the end of the article. The image showed the suspect—this Walter Kneebone fellow—wearing a Texas gentleman's cowboy hat, collared shirt, and bolo tie under a tailored businessman's winter coat.

Grimacing, Rudy considered the appearance of the pasty-faced, thick-jawed individual, then muttered, "That sort of animal should be holdin' hands with Old Nick himself in the hot place, if you ask me." He let out a harrumph, now looking closely at Kneebone's picture. "Looks like me boss's brother back home: same mean eyes . . . close together like bullet holes."

He nodded and looked up at the spattering rain on his windshield. "All men like that got the same black heart! Am I right, Goddess?"

A rumble of thunder overhead broke the sound of steady rain. Then a squelch over the CB radio caught his attention.

"Car Fourteen, come in! Fourteen, come in."

Rudy picked up the mike. "Fourteen here."

"Barabbas!" the dispatch supervisor barked. "Herb's in early. Needs the wheels. Don't drag your feet tonight like you've been doin' the last couple days."

Rudy moved the heel of his boot and bumped the package under his seat. At the same time, he felt a wave of anxiety, and his focus stalled.

"Barabbas!" came the supervisor's voice.

"Oh, uh . . . sure, no problem, boss. Only walking dead out tonight anyway."

Rudy set the mike on top of the newspaper beside him, wanting a moment to think.

They'll break me legs if I miss that 12:15 delivery. Should never have agreed to carry for them.

"Barabbas! You still there?"

Rudy snatched up the mike. "Here, boss."

"You'll never hold another steering wheel in this town if you keep Herb waiting again, got that?"

"No need for threats, boss. You have me word. I'll be in on time."

"Your word don't mean dick, Barabbas! Just don't be late again, or it's your job."

The squelch of the CB punctuated his supervisor's bluntness. Sighing, Rudy replaced the mike and then pulled a faded picture from his pocket. The image showed him and his faraway love, Mala, standing on a pristine Jamaican beach, their arms around each other. A friend had taken the photo on the day Rudy left to make a new life for them in America. Mala's smile was forced; she hadn't been happy about their parting at all.

"She always see the future better den me," Rudy whispered. "How you tell her what you done and make it right?" He turned the key in the ignition and the cab chugged to life. "Mala gonna skin me alive for this."

Flicking on the wipers, Rudy slid the gearshift into drive and pressed the gas pedal. The cab left the puddled curb with an elevated burble and rolled away down the depressing, empty street.

***

The cab had puttered along the rain-glazed street for about a quarter-mile before Rudy shut off the radio's forecast of more rain to come. The traffic light ahead turned red, bringing the cab and Rudy's thoughts to an intersection.

"Give me a sign, Goddess. Rudy's own choices hasn't done him much good of late."

As he sat there at the T intersection waiting for the light to change, a stray dog with gray fur emerged from an alley to his right. It crossed to the center of the road, blocking the right turn, the turn he *should* make back to the Caesar's Cabs depot. The streetlight highlighting the mangy dog began to flicker and then went out, leaving a wall of darkness to the right. Rudy looked left as the traffic light in front of the cab turned green. No obstruction there . . . and a clear-lit path.

Okay, Goddess, he thought. *Rudy sees your meanin'. If this will help make it right for Mala, then that's where we're goin'.*

Rudy turned left—away from the direct route back to base, instead heading in the direction of the drop-off for the package under his seat. Poor personal choices had always overridden Rudy's ability to discriminate well, he knew. But this one . . . well, the Goddess of Rasta had played her part in it.

That had to have good in it, didn't it?

Still, his common sense told him—actually screamed at him—that this choice *was* his point of no return. Rudy pushed the gas harder and the old cab seemed to complain, with the engine missing a beat before picking up again to a dull roar. Now he'd lose his job for sure. Then again, if he didn't deliver the package to the Caracara gang lieutenant on time, as ordered, then he'd lose a lot more than his job. Late or undelivered crew merchandise came at a price, and he stood to be convicted of both.

Another traffic light ahead turned red, and a city patrol car rolled on through in front of Rudy. The rain pounded harder now, making Rudy's wipers splash water over his windshield as if he were in a car wash. He gritted his teeth and pressed the brake pedal to slow and avoid any unwanted attention. His cab came to stop with a short squeal of brakes, adjacent to an old green sedan on the right, with two occupants in the front seat. The glow from the overhead streetlights gave the sedan's occupants a vague suggestion of surly faces, eyes fixed forward.

While Rudy tried not to stare too hard at the people in the sedan, all of the sudden his driver's side rear passenger door popped open. Out of the increasing downpour lunged a passenger, who slammed the door shut with a thump once inside.

"What the . . . ?" Rudy said. "Hey, mon! Me cab's off—"

Rudy choked the rest of   his words down when he saw the face of his
passenger in the rearview mirror.

Oh shit.

He snapped a look down at the newspaper beside him to be sure.

Oh shit.

"I'll pay extra, buddy. Just get me to Beecham Street East!" the man said in a gruff, uncompromising tone.

Fear washed over Rudy. The man looked about forty and sounded out of breath. He was soaked from the rain, but it was him alright—Walter Kneebone.

Rudy felt the hair on the back of his neck stand up.

"Hey!" Kneebone said. "The light's green. Step on it fella!" Then he glanced through his side window to the building opposite . . . as if someone was following close behind him.

Rudy's eyes dropped from the rearview mirror to the road in front. His stomach lurched into a hollow as his mind raced with thoughts about the fare in his backseat.

"Come on, fella, let's go!" Kneebone said. "Beecham Street!" He slapped a hand against his door.

Rudy reached to flag the meter out of habit and then went to press the gas pedal, but put his foot right back on the brakes again. Forming a wall directly in front of the cab, two trucks interrupted the path by rolling through the intersection, running the red light.

Kneebone looked to the building across the way again, and this time Rudy noticed by way of his rearview mirror that his passenger showed a sense of urgency in his expression.

A breath later Rudy's heart jumped when the cab's other rear passenger door opened. A gust of chilled rain and wind blew in, and with it came a dark-haired man in a heavy black coat that covered most of a dark suit beneath.

And then Rudy saw the man's face in the rearview. *Wait, dark glasses at night. Really? Who this guy think he is?*

"Hey, mon, dis cab is taken," Rudy said.

With pale skin and his dark sunglasses, this guy had G-man written all over him. Rudy turned just a bit and saw the new passenger reach out with one hand, grabbing Kneebone's arm—even as Kneebone himself opened his door and attempted to leap out of the cab. The new arrival, though, yanked Kneebone back into the vehicle with unexpected strength.

Rudy felt his eyes go wide as he stared into the rearview mirror and saw the new arrival looking right at him.

"Yes, it is taken," the man said.

Rudy felt an even more intense flush of cold fear creep over him. He watched as the second man turned his eyes toward Kneebone, then Rudy looked ahead again.

"Now, Walter," the man said, "that wasn't sticking to our agreement at all, was it? I can see we didn't make ourselves clear. Let's rectify that, shall we?"

The man in the black coat spoke with a soft, but menacing, educated British accent. His aura exuded intimidation—far greater than even the murderer sitting next to him . . . at least to Rudy. Peeking in his rearview again, Rudy felt an overwhelming urge to flee when he saw that Kneebone—a coldhearted murderer—looked terrified.

Yet Kneebone managed to rally himself and sneer, "I owe you nothing. Nothing! Our agreement is done."

Deciding to flee, Rudy reached for his door handle as the two men struggled in the back. As he leaned on the handle, the struggle behind him stalled. At the same time, Rudy saw ice crystals claw their way around the edge of the windshield glass directly in front of him, and then a voice cut into him from the backseat.

"Move that handle one more inch, cabbie," said the man in the dark coat, "and I'll stretch your skin to reupholster this transport."

Rudy froze. The man's words made his blood run cold. His voice had a final menacing chill to it that made Rudy's jaw tighten.

"Get your meat-hooks off me!" Kneebone shouted, managing to wrestle out of his assailant's grip. "No matter how powerful you are, Insidio, I told you and that evil bitch, no—and it's still no!"

Rudy's mind screamed to escape while his body remained illogically frozen in fear of what might happen should he move another muscle.

The Keyhole Killer is in me cab and afraid of someone worse. Goddess, help me!

Rudy swallowed his rising terror as best he could and turned in his seat to look at his passengers. He smacked the top of the steering wheel with one hand even as the passengers focused their aggression on each other.

"Hey, you two got things to say, take it outside!"

Both individuals in the back swung their view to Rudy, and he immediately wanted to take his words back. The man whom Walter had called "Insidio" shifted his grip to grab a firm fistful of Walter's lapel. With his free hand Insidio pulled the top of his glasses down to expose a pair of lifeless black eyes. To Rudy it felt like looking into some bottomless, painful chasm. His stomach roiled.

"I'll not warn you again, Rudy Barabbas," Insidio said. "Remain still or have your soul core experience pain without end."

Hearing the guy in the black coat call him by name, Rudy gulped. The ultimatum seemed to rip the breath and any independent response straight from his chest. Rudy faced front and sat there as if he were a posed mannequin.

He . . . He spoke me name. How he know me name?

Silent seconds followed, as it appeared this Insidio had Kneebone right where he wanted him, as the killer now said nothing and made no move to escape.

Still wanting to flee, Rudy jumped in his seat when the front passenger door swung open. Against his own will, Rudy turned in that direction.

What the . . . ?

Another sweeping wave of dread washed over him when in slid an attractive brunette with shoulder-length hair. She wore the same dark glasses and coat as the one called Insidio in the back. He could feel her cold stare from behind the dark lenses as she looked him up and down.

"This on the menu too, Insidio?" she asked with the same British accent.

Even a glance told Rudy that she had the kind of curvaceous body every man would desire. The shape of her face was that of an angel—but with the cold expression of something not quite right. She also had the kind of aura which told any male that death by a thousand cuts was sure to follow . . . a death he'd take willingly anyway.

Rudy swallowed hard. A cold smile lined her lips . . . and then all the doors auto-locked at the same time—a feature the cab didn't have. The woman slid across the bench seat toward Rudy. He caught a glimpse of her skirt hitching up a little to expose legs in sheer black stockings. She reached out to touch his face gently with her long nails, and for a snap he thought he saw her lick her lips. Her nails felt like fine razors against his five o'clock shadow.

"I like privacy when I dine," she said to Rudy. "Don't you?" She smiled and then turned toward her associate in the backseat. "This one's yummy. So much good light to drink in. Can't we take him back for dinner? I'm famished." Her intent to satisfy her appetite sounded more sinister than hungry to Rudy.

"Insidia, please stay focused," Insidio said. "We're not here for that. You know we have other more pressing matters to deal with."

The traffic light ahead still showed green. And for some reason, the sedan next to them hadn't moved, but as Rudy looked over at it, hoping to get their attention, it pulled out and left—as if none of the fracas in the cab had been seen.

"Hey!" Rudy bellowed in a futile attempt to draw the sedan's attention.

But the sedan quickly grew small in the distance, leaving his cab isolated at the intersection. Rudy felt a sinking in the pit of his stomach—deserted, left to the whims of some random murderous individuals who had invaded his cab.

What the hell happen now?

Taking a breath to steady himself, Rudy asked, "What do you want?"

The woman lurched even closer to him, overrunning his personal space. Rudy reeled, cracking his head against the door pillar as she rested splayed fingers firmly over his heart. Rudy's eyes bulged, and he remained frozen.

"Tannery, Old Walbash Road," she ordered, removing herself back into the passenger position. "Drive."

Rudy still had the chill of her in his bones even though she had withdrawn, and his limbs refused to respond.

Eyes remaining forward, Insidia placed one long-nailed finger on her lips. She removed her glasses, displaying her own pair of jet-black eyes before saying softly, "Either you use this transport to take us where we need to be, Rudy Barabbas, or I see how far your entrails will stretch around its circumference."

Rudy's eyes darted forward. He pressed the accelerator and the cab burbled on into the night.

***

The cab rolled along the gloom of Old Walbash Road toward the tannery. The familiarity of the road he'd traveled many times—and the reasons for doing so —only added to Rudy's present living nightmare, one he desperately wanted escape from. This end of town was much older, with closed factories and untidy vacant lots. As the cab drove onward, groups of people could be seen huddled around fire barrels, sheltered in alleys. Some sang while others just shivered against the wet and cold. On two occasions Rudy was sure he saw that stray gray dog he'd seen at the intersection: once while passing an alleyway, and another time beside a Dumpster near a street corner with a single light.

The mood in his cab felt beyond dark; it was downright eerie. Even the cab seemed to be traveling quieter so as not to upset any of the passengers within. Rudy mused that putting his funeral arrangements together would have been a happier event.

Wait, maybe there's something in that. He wanted to look at the ice maiden on his right, but he dare not. The way she sat there ... *How do someone sit there like evil incarnate and not be doing anything except the sitting?* It was as if even though her eyes were looking to the road ahead, Rudy felt she'd never taken her attention off him for a second during their entire journey.

He started to hum a little tune to push away the anxiety. Insidia turned her gaze slowly in his direction. He stopped humming and she turned her view back to the horizon. *Oh, the Caracara boys—especially Mr. Manny—not gonna take this intrusion well at all.*

But then Manny Caracara didn't like anything that wasn't his idea, at any time.

The headlights of the cab peeped over the crest of a small rise, pointing directly out of town. Nothing was out here. Nothing except the place they were heading to.

CHAPTER

2

Home This Isn't

People don't call this end of town "the Dead End" for no good reason, Rudy thought.

He knew the old tannery on Walbash well. He'd had occasion to drive up there several times in the last two weeks. It was at the far end of the road they were now on. At this juncture the road began to ascend to higher ground heading into the hills. The frigid, sheeting rain had finally relented, but the cold still bit to the bone, and the cab's heater struggled to improve things. Rudy noticed that the bleak weather seemed to have no effect on the woman beside him, or the others in the back for that matter.

Then the radio squelched.

"Fourteen! Fourteen, come in," the shift supervisor said. "Barabbas! Where are you! I'll have your balls on a plate if you're not here in sixty seconds."

Rudy went to lean forward and take the mike. But Insidia's action froze him back in place with both hands on the wheel. She placed one finger on the black edge of the mike. It shorted with a spark that made Rudy jump a little.

She looked at Rudy. "Your balls, sweetheart, now belong to me."

"Believe me, kid," said Kneebone from the backseat. "The bitch is capable of far worse than that."

Insidia smiled at Rudy in a way that had the hair on his neck standing again, and then she casually turned her view back to the road ahead. Rudy swallowed, continuing to point the cab in the direction of the old tannery.

****

The sandy road shoulder and embankments leading to their destination looked badly eroded. It was clear they hadn't seen attention for some time. The cab's headlights shifted from one inner raw-banked corner to the gravel knife-edge cliff of the next. The shoulder lacked any guardrail. Rudy's stomach held tight with growing trepidation. Who were Insidia and Insidio, and what lay ahead?

Rudy noticed Insidia reach for something from inside her jacket. She studied a strange object about the size of a cigarette packet. It appeared to be some kind of technology with lights and a small screen. She tapped at something on the screen with one sharp fingernail. The device could have been straight out of Dick Tracy's world of wristwatch communicators and space radios.

"Have we been detected?" asked Insidio from the backseat.

Insidia shrugged. "There was one anomaly a short while ago. But I couldn't get a lock on the signature long enough to determine off-worlder or solid dirt-sider."

Rudy looked in his rearview and noticed Insidio looking out the back window.

"I don't like the feel of it," Insidio said. "We'll need to be clinical on this one."

"No time for a stopover, then?" Insidia asked.

Rudy saw Insidio shake his head. "Afraid not, old girl," he said. "We'll need to move on the moment we've cleaned up Walter's mess to avoid any unnecessary chance meetings."

Insidia looked at Rudy. "Pity."

Rudy felt her stare boring into him. He tried not to look at the creepy ice maiden next to him for fear she might just want to snack on him. But he found his view dragged to her momentarily anyway. Having such an attractive view close by ordinarily made him forget any stress. This one, though, gave him the shivers.

She picked up the newspaper between them and took in the article about Walter with a little mocking laugh before looking back at the killer.

"I told you, Insidio," she said. "There was no way he'd follow through this last time. We should have traded him after that last agreement."

"Hey, you black-eyed bitch," Walter snapped. "I did everything we agreed! You owe me my life back at end of business before midnight tonight. You never said anything about added extras in our contract. Knew you'd both welsh, paradin' around like some limy duke and duchess. I goddamn knew it! The other side will find you two again, just like the time before."

"You've said quite enough, Walter," Insidia said.

"What are you gonna do," Walter continued, "replace me with the chump in the front?"

An awkward silence filled the inside of the cab.

Insidia looked at Rudy. "Walter has a point, you know. His soul core is nearly depleted from retaining the Darkness Strings needed. We'll need a new physical world anchor soon anyway. Once we reacquire the module that's fallen into our target's hands with the payload of the high-grade crystal to charge our cyclonic transfer module, we can get off this primitive world and finish our mission. The moment I get my hands on her, I'm going to skin that agent of Zero's and hurl her mass into the nearest sun."

Rudy just blinked and focused on the road in front of him. *The cyclonic trans-what? Agents? What mission?* His head raced to grasp any thread of her meaning.

Then in the rearview he saw Walter wipe his neck with a handkerchief taken from an inside coat pocket.

"Hey, you guys, come on," said Walter, an obvious edge of concern scratching through his voice. "I . . . I was jokin', okay? You see that . . . right?" He forced a smile before a dissatisfied scowl replaced his false expression.

Neither Insidio nor Insidia responded.

"Fine, then,' Walter said. "You need me while your feet have shoes on the ground and you know it."

Rudy watched Insidio glare at Walter deadpan—long enough for Walter to have to fidget.

Way to go, bonehead!

"It's because of your cock-up earlier, Walter," Insidio said.

Who woulda guessed?

"Now *we* find ourselves in this predicament and pressed for time," said Insidia, glaring at Walter from the front seat.

Insidio leaned in a little closer to Walter. "Things are at stake far beyond your small Earth-life comprehension."

"I know more than you two think," Walter said.

"Yes," said Insidio calmly, "we've considered that. We may address it later. We made a simple bargain, Walter. We dug you out of a rather sticky predicament with some very determined dirt-side law enforcement. In return we asked for a small favor, and we had your agreement swiftly, I seem to remember. We take those agreements seriously, Walter. We supplied you with a karmic-debt short list to attend to. We were pleased with your progress, until this last matter. Your final task was simple: help acquire the witness nominated and the messenger bound to circumstance in question. Then retrieve and plant the diamonds as directed with your business associate to . . . throw a cat in with the chickens. Did I say it right?"

"No, you limey-faced bastard. It's 'a cat amongst the pigeons,' see?" said Walter with sarcasm and some satisfaction at winning a point.

"You were supposed to remove the daughter of those indebted to us and then rough her up a bit to make the deal sweet," Insidio went on. "Make a call and send a photo, and then leave the rest to us. Why at this juncture in our contract would you renege, Walter? You're almost home free."

"I told you," Walter said. "I don't do teenage girls, carrying a delivery or not. It's too twisted . . . bad for my ulcer. I tried to wrestle 'em off of her, but the kid got away with the package and ran straight back to her mother."

The cab jarred at hitting a double pothole in the road. The bump and bounce caused Walter to wince and hold his side in clear discomfort.

"Christ, bonehead!" Walter snapped, glaring up toward Rudy. "Keep this thing straight!"

"Sorry," Rudy said.

"Stay focused, Walter," Insidio said. "So you went there and slit the throat of the mother instead. Fool! That gave us no choice but to intervene. That woman's untimely passing gained the interest of some of our opposition that we can't have near our present dealings. Have I made myself clear?"

Walter shrugged. "She got in the way. I had to shut her up. Like I said, the bitch deserved it! She told me some shit story about some other guy there earlier. He asked for the package. She called me a jerk-off. Said to go chase him. Said she gave the package to him, happy to see the back of it. I found that schmuck, and he said he gave it to a spade."

Rudy remembered being handed the package—the very one that sat under his seat right now. The delivery guy told him not to look at the contents, and he hadn't.

"Bitch tried to slam the door in my face," Walter said. "Warning *me* she knew some bad people. Threatened me with what her old man would do if I touched either of them. I knew who she meant. The threat meant nothin'. You told me no witnesses so . . . I did what I had to." Walter looked up toward Rudy. "And now there's a delivery boy—this spade—to dump too. That's right, Rudy Barabbas, I know who you are. Where did you put the package, huh?"

Rudy swallowed the lump in his throat and spoke slowly to calm himself. "I got no idea what you're talking about, mon. I drive a cab. Don't know anything about no package of diamonds."

Walter snorted a laugh. "Oh, it's you, spade. We both know it's you."

"I see light from a building in the distance," Insidia said.

"That's the place, that's the place!" said Rudy, glad to change the subject.

Insidio slapped Walter's face and then spoke through gritted teeth. "Listen to me, you idiot. Stop with all the redirect. These are no ordinary diamonds. In fact they are not diamonds at all. If our cabbie here had what we seek, he'd have been tainted the moment he looked upon them and we'd smell it a mile off."

Walter harrumphed. "Get this, Insidio. I don't care what you do to me. I'm not getting caught in any screwed-up crossfire. I smell a rat and it's sittin' in the front seat."

Now Walter lashed out with a fist and thumped the back of Rudy's seat.

"You want a decoy," Walter said, "then use the goddamn spade. Whatever you want from Manny, you get it yourself."

Rudy used his heel to again bump the roll of contraband under his seat. A flush of cold ran through him.

Goddess, no! he thought. *It couldn't be the same bag some woman much earlier today found and handed over to one of her dodgy Caracara cousins. The same guy who then handed the bag to me for delivery.* Rudy swallowed. *Could it be?*

"Don't worry, Rudy Barabbas," said Insidia, not looking at him, "it will all be at an end soon."

"They're something your small Earth-bound brain would only fail to grasp the true value of," Insidio said to Walter. "Without them I'm afraid you could be enjoying our company indefinitely."

"Fuck that!" said Walter.

"Yes, quite," Insidio said. "Something that displeases Insidia and me just as much, I can assure you. You've killed an innocent with no negative karmic debt, you imbecile. Alarm bells all the way to Juno Bridgeport in the M System Core of the Superverse will have been rung."

"How far to our destination, Rudy Barabbas?" Insidia asked.

Rudy cleared his throat. "Umm . . . just up the road a bit—a couple minutes more."

Insidia gave a quick nod. "Good. The stench of weakness in this transport is beginning to annoy me."

"Look, Insidio," Walter went on. "All I want is the end of this deal, see? When it's done, I'm out of here. That's what we agreed."

"Oh, you so are out of here, little man," said Insidia, turning to glare at him.

Insidio sneered. "Your incompetence has ensured that the Citadel Council will already have dispatched an investigator . . . something we can well do without. The last thing we need is a Citadel Council warden turning up to poke their nose in. Perhaps I should have let Insidia do as she would like—and then started afresh. Hmm . . . We still could, I suppose. There are other potential suitors newly arrived on offer. But, fortunately for you, Walter, we are stuck with this course for now. You'll see things through if you want to enjoy another life cycle. Do I make myself clear?"

"Yeah, yeah, I heard you," Walter said.

The heavy silence that followed drenched Rudy with foreboding until Insidio spoke again.

"Your untidy treatment of the objective has forced us into the open, Walter. We are compelled to take harsher measures now. Just hold your nerve and the course intended will be self-correcting."

Insidia had been observing the exchange with her head turned toward the backseat, but now she angled her attention to Rudy. He felt her reach across and place her hand on his thigh. He cringed at the coldness of the contact, unable to repel her. She gave him a wicked little smile.

"Don't worry, Golliwog," she said. "You're important to me now. No one will harm you without my permission. I want you all to myself."

He gripped the steering wheel with both hands and dared not look at her.

She chuckled. "Why, Rudy Barabbas, the smell of fear is all over you! Who would have thought?"

Rudy took a deep breath. Insidia gave him a cynical smile before looking away to the shadows and bleak unfolding nightscape. Rudy wondered about his chances of bailing out around the next bend.

But what if something's coming the other way?

A sheet of rain slapped the windshield, reinforcing the absurdity of such an attempt.

Yeah, but it still be worth a try considering me present company, he considered.

Without turning his head Rudy slid his eyes to the right. Insidia appeared to be paying him no attention.

Alright then.

He dropped his hand casually to the door handle and applied pressure to it as the cab came onto a stretch of straight road. The door handle refused to budge. His jaw tightened.

Fuck!

Into his mind came the unnerving image of the doors locking themselves earlier.

Fuck! FUCK!

He cast a quick sideways glance at her again.

"Don't worry, Golliwog!" said Insidia, monotone and not looking at him. "I'll tell you when it's time to get out."

"Get out of me head, woman!"

Insidia turned her gaze squarely upon him. At the same time, from the backseat Insidio said, "Be happy Insidia is in a pleasant mood, Rudy. You wouldn't like her darker side at all."

Darker side? Goddess, save me!

He slung a glance her way to see one corner of her full red lips lift in a tiny curl to create a wicked smile. He felt her eyes boring into him from behind those lenses before she switched her gaze back to the road ahead. Rudy was sure she'd smiled at his failure.

"You know the tannery will likely be closed in all this bad weather," Rudy said.

He hoped the lie tumbling awkwardly from his lips might press them to an alternative.

"They'll be open for business," Walter said. "Manny's boys just about live there."

Reluctantly Rudy pointed the cab into a steady right turn where the pavement faded to gravel. Directly in front of them loomed the uneven, grim façade of the old tannery, which at one time had also doubled as a slaughterhouse. With the facility deliberately built far outside of town, none of San Antonio's residents had been exposed to all the butchering over the years. In this factory of death, thousands of beasts had regularly met their untimely end. Apparently so had many a crooked and sometimes blameless individual.

Rudy released pressure on the gas pedal and began to apply the brakes. The occupants of the cab could hear the wheels of their transport groan to a halt in the wet gravel. Before them stood the front gates of a place that had been there since the Prohibition years. The run-down complex hulked in the darkness liked something straight out of a B-grade horror movie. A cluster of three substantial buildings had served the various uses of a slaughterhouse. In the far background to the right were the old stockyard pens. There, beasts would have been kept to await a merciless death.

The complex stood blanketed in mist under a just-breaking cloud that allowed filtered moonlight to illuminate the grim setting. Red security signs boldly warned: *"Danger"* . . . *"Keep Out"* . . . *"Dog Patrols."* On either side of the wide front gates, a tall, rusty security fence framed the signage and traced a forbidding perimeter that disappeared like an ink line into the distance. At first no sign of life could be detected from outside. A pathetic light outside the entrance of a small outer building drew the attention of the cab's occupants.

"See," Walter said. "I told you. Manny is always open for business."

CHAPTER

3

Tighten the Noose

Unconsciously Rudy pressed himself harder into the seat, wanting to avoid the displeasure of driving through the gates—something he had been compelled to do several times before. Vince Caracara, one of Manny Caracara's sons, had caught Rudy trying to stack the odds at a dice game a couple of months back. Herb, on the B shift for Caesar's Cabs, had introduced Rudy to the game. But Rudy had pushed his luck, lost big, and couldn't come up with the cash. So a favor was owed to pay the debt. That's all it took. Failure to comply meant broken hands or shins or both. And Vince clearly enjoyed his work. He'd told Rudy before the first delivery job, "Do this one thing and all would be forgiven." Not so. Vince had also said he'd make the deliveries worth Rudy's while. Not so. Finally Vince had said Rudy would get everything due to him after the very next delivery. Definitely so . . . if Rudy lucked out tonight. Now the weight of that package seemed to lean heavier against his boot heel.

"Sound the horn, stupid," Walter said. "You know the drill. Or else you'll make someone nervous in there, which I don't recommend."

Rudy hit the horn twice and waited.

Shuffling in the backseat, Walter said, "Look, Insidio, you've got everything you wanted. Things worked out, didn't they? I found you the mark you're *really* after, didn't I? You don't need me now."

"Too late," said Insidio.

As he said it, an individual in a trench coat opened the gate and waved them inside.

The cab passed by the guy holding the gate, wheels splashing through random puddles.

"Something you're not telling us, Walter?" Insidio asked.

"Nah, Manny and I had a little disagreement couple days ago, that's all. He might not be as . . . approachable as usual when he sees it's me with guests."

"So what is it you tell the others in your little syndicate, Walter?" Insidio asked. "Don't bullshit a bullshitter?"

Rudy took a slow breath and brought the cab to a halt again. All the occupants looked toward the aging gray frontage of the tannery's business entrance. A small metal shade protected the single lightbulb over the door, barely providing enough illumination to highlight the entrance. A boarded-up window could be seen to the left. Rudy noticed a thread of light bleeding through its cracks from inside. To the right of the building, three black limousines stood parked in the shadows.

Really don't want to be goin' in der, Rudy thought.

All four door locks popped simultaneously, which made him jump.

"Okay," Rudy said. "No charge for the trip, mon. It's been fun, so you all have a good night, den."

Cold, heavy silence met his statement. Rudy turned to his right and forced his best smile at Insidia, still hoping to be released.

Insidia ignored him and looked into the back at Walter. "Okay, Walter, we're *all* going inside."

Rudy blinked and felt his heart sink—then watched as Insidio reached toward Walter's abdomen. He inserted his entire hand through the fabric of Walter's clothes and deep into the flesh behind. As Walter's eyes widened with the wave of immense pain that surely followed, Rudy felt himself trembling.

"Once we're in there," said Insidio, seeming to enjoy the moment, "you identify the mark by speaking to them first, Walter. We'll take care of the rest. We are agreed, I hope."

Walter groaned in obvious pain, and Rudy faced forward again.

"Try to run on us this time," said Insidio, "and Insidia will have free rein over any painful pleasure she wishes to inflict upon you."

Rudy heard another painful groan, and then what sounded like something wet being extracted.

"Alright, alright, goddamn it!" Walter replied, breathing a loud sigh of relief.

"Good," Insidia said. "Knew you'd see it our way." Then she looked at Rudy. "You will be accompanying us too, Rudy Barabbas."

Still feeling himself shiver all over, Rudy glanced into the back of the cab to see how bad Walter's injuries were. Astonishingly, Walter appeared unharmed, except for a fading incandescence over his sternum.

"Under your seat," said Insidia, drawing Rudy's attention again, "there is a package."

Rudy's shoulders fell, his head dropped, and he nodded.

"Carefully reach down, avoid contact with the weapon hidden there, and respectfully hand the package to me."

Rudy's eyes widened and he hesitated. *Nobody knows about me Hardballer under me seat, mon! How the hell did she—*

"I'd do it now, Rudy!" Insidio said the backseat.

Rudy complied, finally placing the rolled package into Insidia's waiting hand. She smiled glibly at him. As he sat back, he looked past her, through the passenger window, at the front door of the tannery. There, to the right of the door, he noticed a heavyset individual in a black hat and coat standing on the edge of the soft light. The misting rain and shadow gave him a sinister look. Rudy had seen him here before but never caught his name.

"Better get movin'," Walter said. "Manny's boys never like being kept waiting. Something Manny especially has a thing about. That goon you can see over there—just a distraction. If you don't move, very soon someone will—"

Rudy barely had time to turn his head as each door of the cab opened to the rain-soaked night. Four men dressed in coats and hats for wet weather seemed to have come from nowhere. They held the doors open in silence.

The one standing close to Rudy held a pistol-grip pump-action shotgun in one hand, barrel pointing to the ground. Looking directly at Rudy, he said, "You first, spade," he said. "Everybody else out steady like. State your business. I hope for your sake it's important."

Rudy had his eyes locked on the gunman next to his door. A brief silence followed before Insidia's voice broke in: "My kind of party!"

The goon lifted the barrel of his gun toward Rudy's face. "Don't make me ask again, spade."

Walter and Rudy stepped out of their side of the cab at the same time. Rudy's belly brushed the muzzle of the gunman's weapon, which made him shuffle to one side. Insidia and Insidio exited on the other side of the cab, covered by a second gunman.

"Hey, mon, point that thing somewhere else," Rudy said. "I'm just deliverin' me fare."

The shotgun-toting goon looked to the entrance. "Whatcha wanna do, Fritz?"

The individual previously on the edge of shadow stepped in to the light. He considered the new arrivals.

"No spades inside!" he said. His hoarse voice suggested a life of smoke-filled nightclubs and seedy bars. "The boss ain't gonna . . . Hey, wait a minute! I know you. Mr. Vince is lookin' for you. Ooo, he's not happy! You got balls comin' here after what you pulled."

Rudy's jaw dropped at the accusation. "What *I* pulled! I did exactly what I was told to and . . ."

Rudy's words stalled when he saw Insidia walk around the car. As she approached Rudy, her feminine sway drew the goon's attention. She threaded her arm through Rudy's and smiled at Fritz. Her touch made Rudy's skin crawl.

"It's alright, handsome," Insidia said to Fritz, stepping confidently toward him with a reluctant Rudy in tow. "He's important to our meeting with your boss."

"That's far enough, dolly bird," said Fritz, barring the way. "I decide what's important and what's not."

Insidia glared at him, clearly thinking about her next move.

"Hey, Fritz," Walter said, drawing everyone's attention. "Your eyes still giving you trouble? You're not wearin' those glasses I arranged for you! What's with all the attitude?"

Rudy watched Fritz's expression soften as his attention zeroed in on Walter.

"Mr. Kneebone?" Fritz said. "Didn't see it was you."

"Well, now you do," Walter said. "We need to speak to Manny. Urgent business. These guys are with me. *Including* the spade."

"Boss has important matters tonight, Mr. Kneebone." Fritz gestured to a group of limousines off to the right. "By invite only. Sorry. I got no notice of extra guests on the slate. I'll tell Manny you dropped by."

Fritz's words fell cold and final. Walter shook his head and the trajectory of the covering goon's gun barrel drifted Walter's way. Walter looked awkwardly to Insidia and back to Fritz. "Aw, come on, Fritz, it's cold out here. Manny is gonna want to hear what my associates have to say real bad. It's directly connected to business they are discussing in there tonight."

"I told you!" Fritz said. "Mr. Caracara is in conference with the board. Give me the info. I'll pass it on, or come back another time."

Rudy watched Walter roll his eyes and look skyward. Clearly exasperated, Walter took a deep breath.

"For Christ's sake, Fritz. You're not hearing me. It's the meeting we are here about. I got through to Manny at the last minute." Walter gestured toward Rudy. "I have somethin' that'll help ease your boss's ulcer. Took awhile to round these guys up. So don't make us later than we already are."

Fritz gave them all a steady cold stare and slid a hand into one of his coat's deep pockets, which made Rudy think he'd taken hold of a piece to finish the discussion.

After a couple of moments, Fritz shrugged. He looked at his gunmen. "Stand down. Okay then, Mr. Kneebone, it's your funeral. Little Vince, escort the late guests inside."

Little Vince—the one with the shotgun—gestured for Insidio, still waiting on the other side of the cab, to join them. Rudy's mouth felt full of cotton over what was to come. His flight instinct held full throttle, and just when he thought to make a break for it, he felt Insidia's fingers pass right through the material of his coat and bond cold to the flesh of his arm. He whimpered.

"Stay with me, Golliwog," he heard Insidia say inside his head. *"It'll all be over soon."*

Fritz leveled his gaze on Insidia. "Spade can wait in the barn where they used to keep all the animals."

"Fritz. Is *that* your name?" Insidia asked. "You don't know me, but I'm here to do your boss a big favor. You have a boss from up north in there—a Mr. Sabastian, yes? And another man—a Mr. Beck, right?"

Fritz nodded. "Yeah, that's right. Unlike you, they're on the list. What's it to ya?"

"I work for Mr. Beck. This is one of Mr. Beck's informants." She tilted her head toward Rudy.

Fritz eyed Rudy cautiously and shook his head.

"Listen carefully, meat-for-brains," Insidia went on. "You have your job and I have mine, I get it. But there is about to be a coup inside. Your boss, and mine, and a lot of people in there, will die if you don't let us intervene."

"I dunno, little lady. It'll be my hide if you're not straight with this."

"Look, pie-face, you can double-tap my chest with that little .38 you're holding in your pocket the moment I'm proven false. Mr. Sabastian in there has a very nasty surprise planned for your boss and mine. They need to hear what we have to say—now!" As if to emphasize her point, she reached out and squeezed Fritz's arm. "Or you'll be looking to join a new crew real soon."

With her words and contact, Fritz staggered a step, suddenly looking pale. "Okay, okay, but I'll remember you. Broads don't take that tone with me." With that Fritz reached for the doorknob and gestured for them to enter. "Good luck."

CHAPTER

4

Powder Keg

Inside the next room Little Vince gestured to another door at the back of a reception office that wasn't much more than a counter and a telephone. Beyond that door the murmurings of voices could be heard. Little Vince passed by Rudy and opened the door into a much more substantial room. This part of the complex, which Rudy had heard of but never seen, made the hair on the back of his neck stand up. The ominous space, originally a product display room, had been repurposed as the Caracara boardroom. Its atmosphere offered no comfort. Sample hides hung on the wall, reinforcing the true purpose of the facility: death. The group walked on through into a tense atmosphere, with the door closing silently behind them.

***

Fifteen of the Caracara cartel's core family faced off in two groups. They sat around a large oak boardroom table laden with beverages—red wine by first glance—and what appeared to be the remains of a light supper. Plumes of cigarette smoke that hung gray above the men swirled under two long florescent lights. At the end of the table, farthest from the door, sat Manny Caracara, head of the family. Though now confined to a wheelchair, his ruthless control of the family business and everything connected to it remained undiminished.

Rudy suddenly heard Insidia inside his head again: *"That's Beck and Sabastian at the far end on the right."*

Figuring he should answer, Rudy thought, *"Manny Caracara is in the wheelchair."*

"Good, I can clean two messes up at once," he heard Insidia reply.

Oh Goddess! Rudy thought to himself.

Insidia looked to Rudy and whispered, "She can't help you now."

Unexpectedly Rudy felt her attention shift to each member of the group at the table in turn. *What does she want here?* he wondered to himself.

"It's more of a 'who,'" she answered in Rudy's mind. *"The old man will do for starters."*

Rudy considered Manny and the way he presided over what was clearly a tense discussion at the table—so tense that no one had even noticed them come in yet. Rudy knew the ruthless reputation Manny had for dealing with things labeled as obstacles. It never ended well for the obstacle. They all watched Manny's two sons, Vince and Albert, wrestle verbally over differences in controlling the family business.

"Pop, Al," said Vince. "Like I said, I brought these two gentlemen into this meeting to reassure you both that everything was fine with our new alliance in the north. Everything *is* above board."

From his seat the broad-shouldered Albert shook his head. "Above board!" He poked a finger toward his younger brother. "Vince, I told you not to trust outsiders with such responsibility—ever."

"Al, let me ask you," Vince said, "is this any way to show the north how we do business?"

The tiniest curl of a sneer lifted Albert's lip. "Look, Vince, I've had that damn cop and his crew on my ass for days over this. You better clean this mess up or there'll be a reckoning."

Vince threaded a hand of manicured fingers through a head of thick hair. He stood with a sullen expression of his own before resting his hands on the table. "A reckoning," Vince finally said. "Look around, big brother! Our friends from up north are here because they have concerns about our ability to get things done." Vince looked at Beck and Sabastian confidently. "Am I right?"

The two out-of-towners nodded.

"Thank you," Vince said. "Nice to see there are *some* clear heads at this table." Looking emboldened by their support, Vince swung his gaze back to his brother. "Ever since Pop's sickness got worse, things have gone to hell and deeper with you and your 'new strategy.' We are losing respect for everything we've built on the streets here. Soon people will get it into their head that they can choose to do what they want. Then what's next? They'll start in on our turf, that's what. All that stupid cabbie had to do was make a delivery on time. If he'd done like he was told, those stupid cops would have cleaned up the opposition for us. That friggin' judge would have been right where we wanted him. All in one sweep, that do-gooder cop would have been finished too." Vince patted his chest. "Us in the clear!"

Vince turned to his father. "Pop, you can see what I was tryin' to do here, right?"

Gaunt faced and breathing hard with a wheezy cough, the old man looked from one son to the other. He dabbed his mouth with a handkerchief. "Stop pointin' blame and start fixin' the problem. Find the spade. Recover the package. Ensure that our new partners in the north are given the respect they deserve, and take that cop and his wife on a road trip. Then let's get back to business, okay?"

As everyone gave silent nods, Manny's gaze went to the far end of the room —where Rudy and the others stood.

"What's with the whore and jazz band?" Manny asked. "Party's not till later."

Now everyone's attention turned to Rudy and the new arrivals. Concerned expressions formed on each man's face as Walter Kneebone emerged from behind. Insidia pressed the dreadlock-headed cabbie forward.

Goddess, help me now!

"Ah. It's okay, Pop," Vince said. "The entourage I don't know—yet." Then he gave a nasty little smile. "But this is actually the spade I've been waiting for. Now everything can be cleared up."

Rudy had taken note of Vince Caracara the moment he'd walked in. The sight of the vicious, ice-eyed criminal again had made him shudder with fear. Yet nothing compared to the bone-chilling feeling of having Insidia's other-worldly talons hold him fast. Somehow Rudy knew that even Lucifer Morning Star himself would find it hard to match the capacity for ruthless brutality and mayhem that Insidia could dispense. So he just stood there, trying to avoid eye contact with most everyone.

With the lethal aura of a serial killer pressing at his back, a she-devil fused to his arm, and her accomplice on the other side, Rudy had no escape. If that wasn't bad enough, in front of him sat the murderous cartel that wanted him punished for failure to comply with instructions—a reminder to any who dared ignore a Caracara directive. Everything in Rudy's being told him to flee, but Insidia's grip ensured that was impossible. A cold moment filled the room.

Behind his group Rudy heard the door open and close again. He turned to see the heavyset Fritz standing there and glaring at them with unfeeling eyes. Fritz used a free hand to flick the door lock, which made a soft but final click. Now they were locked in as well. Fritz's other hand remained buried in his coat pocket, still pointing the barrel of the deadly piece he'd had on them outside. He stood there, silent, covering the only apparent exit. Bringing his view back to the men at the table, Rudy saw a satisfied smirk spreading across Vince's expression.

"Well, look what else the wind just blew in along with the spade: Walter, my favorite town engineer—and . . . friends."

"Brought you someone I heard you were looking for," said Walter, pushing Rudy roughly on the shoulder.

Vince nodded with a grin like a man who'd just won big on the ponies. "Rudy Barabbas, I'm very happy to see that black face of yours." Vince looked at the others around the table. "Gentlemen, Pop. If you'll indulge me a little longer, I think we can clear up matters very quickly."

Rudy attempted to swallow with spit he didn't have.

Vince eyed Rudy. "Your absence at the appointed time gave me cause for concern, my cabbie friend."

"It's not me fault, mon!" Rudy said, struggling under the constant tension of Insidia's grip. "The boss switched cabs on me at the last minute. It took more time than I had to find it and get your stuff back while no one was watchin'."

"Really?" Vince said, looking around at the others at the table. He stopped to stare coldly at Beck and Sabastian. "That why one of my crew saw you enterin' the Jack of Diamonds, huh? Instead of deliverin' the package straight to me—*after* you picked up your ride."

Rudy shook his head. "No, mon, that's not—"

"You went to have a conversation with some *new* friends, I see." Vince looked to Kneebone. "What's goin' on, Walter? What're you playin' at?"

"Hey, I've done you a favor here," Walter said.

"No, Vince, that's not what happened, mon," Rudy cut in. "I was on me way here when—"

"Shut up!" Vince said. "I'll tell you all what just happened. You walk in here uninvited, and *both* of you straight to my face start lyin'. That's what just happened. You two have that much disrespect?"

"Hey, wait a minute!" Walter said. He turned his gaze to the old man. "Manny, please tell them, he's got this all wrong!"

"Uh . . ." Rudy said, raising his free hand like a school kid wanting the teacher's attention.

"Shut up!" Vince snarled and stepped toward them. "You're both lyin' pieces of garbage! Where's the damn package?"

"Here it is," Insidia said.

As she said it, she tossed the package to Vince. He caught it awkwardly, clearly surprised.

"You should choose your errand boys and associates with more care, Mr. Caracara," Insidia said. Then she looked at Beck and asked, "Is everything okay, boss?"

"Yeah, Sidia, we're fine. Finish what you came to say," said the red-headed mob boss.

Insidia nodded and then stared at Vince. "I've been following your mule for some time." She gave Rudy a jerk on the arm. "He's taken us to some interesting places. With the help of Mr. Kneebone here, we've been able to form a clear picture of the jeopardy you've been placing everyone in, Mr. Caracara."

"Watch your mouth, bitch, or there'll be consequences," Vince said.

"Then I'll speak slowly for you, Mr. Caracara, so there is no misinterpretation."

Eyes wide, Vince reeled at being spoken to in such a manner by a woman, but before he could say anything, Insidia went on.

"Word on the street is, *you* set up a lot of trusted people both here and in the north to take a fall with these diamonds . . . including your older brother."

Insidia swung her gaze to Albert.

"What the hell?" Albert said.

Vince put up a hand. "Don't listen to her, Al. She's just tryin' to throw us off. Beck, you gonna let your bitch off the leash like that? No broad talks to me that way. I'll have her turned into pet food!"

"Careful, Vince," Beck said. "Sidia's very good at her job, and she never lies."

Beck made his comment while looking straight at the old man in the wheelchair. Manny shifted in his seat to fix his view on Insidia.

"Let the broad speak," Manny said.

"Thank you, Mr. Caracara," Insidia said, smiling. "We merely bring the truth for you and our employer to consider along with this collection of gentlemen. Perhaps there is now a way forward and debts can be settled."

"Truth . . . debts," Vince said, reaching into his pocket. "What is this lady talking about? I'll give you truth." He took a step back from the table and began to take his hand out of his pocket.

"Vince!" Manny snapped, forcing his son to a halt.

Then Manny burst into a spluttering cough, which drew everyone's attention.

"Pop, relax, I got this," Albert said in a soft but serious voice. He looked at his brother. "You know the house rules, Vince. Sit down—now, brother . . . before things get any more awkward."

Vince cast a glare at Insidia and finally moved to his chair. All the men around the table still looked plenty uneasy to Rudy.

"Now, you—little lady with the smart mouth," Albert said to Insidia. "You're stirring up quite a wasp's nest with your accusations. Fritz, put mop-head in the back room. I'll deal with him later."

Fritz moved toward Rudy, slapping a large, meaty hand around the back of his neck. Insidia let Rudy go, and for reasons he couldn't explain to himself, Rudy wasn't sure he wanted her to. Fritz marched Rudy to a door in the shadows to the right. He opened the door and shoved Rudy inside the dark space. Rudy stumbled forward and hit the floor with a crash and groan.

Dis just not good at all.

***

Fritz shut and bolted the door, and then gave Albert a nod.

"Now," Albert said. "Before Mr. Beck's employee speaks further, I want to hear from Mr. Kneebone. Walter, where do you and the suits fit in to all this?"

"Manny, please," Walter said to the old man, ignoring Albert. "Like I said, I heard you were lookin' for the spade. Consider the delivery a gesture of goodwill. These two had an interest in the same individual. I didn't know they worked for Mr. Beck until now. We crossed paths just today. I was seeing to some of that business we discussed last week regarding the delivery. Seems the spade has been doin' some planning of his own for reasons I'm *sure* Fritz here will be able to determine quickly. The woman mentioned something I knew you would find important. It's crucial to a deal Vince was going to use to transfer power of your organization to him." Walter cut his eyes at Vince, then said, "To save any further embarrassment to anyone, please, may I have a moment with head of the family in private?"

Manny looked grimly at his sons and then to the others around the table, halting at Beck and Sabastian. They didn't look pleased at all.

"You got about ten seconds to explain in front of everyone, Walter," Manny said. "It better be good."

***

Inside the old room Rudy could see most of the details by the light of the moon filtering through boards lining the wall opposite. Although the space had the feel of a storeroom, it had clearly been converted to something entirely different. The floor under his hands felt cold and he realized he had fallen onto a sheet of plastic. There was an old table off to one side and a rug covering the floor under it. He also noticed what appeared to be an unused roll of plastic leaning against the wall in the corner. A second untidy roll of it lay on the ground nearby.

With a whimper he tried to stand, but his foot slipped on something slick and he went back down. Rolling up onto a now bruised hip, Rudy noticed his arm was wet. Then, looking hard at the floor, he noticed he was lying in a drying pool of blood. His eyes followed a broad smear of it leading over to the plastic roll on the floor. His stomach lurched at seeing two bloody feet protruding from the end of the roll. Some of the toes were missing.

"Oh, Goddess! Oh no!"

He started to hyperventilate.

CRACK!

The sound of a heavy fist striking timber out in the boardroom made Rudy's heart jump. He clasped his chest as adrenaline coursed through his system.

"I said, NO!" Manny's words punched through the wall almost as hard as his fist had hit the table.

Moving to the door, Rudy peered through a knothole in one of the panels. Through it he had a partial view of the group around the table. Something had changed. He could feel the hostility in the room escalating. Heated words from the exchange sent a clear warning.

Aware, trouble coming.

Rudy saw Insidia ignore the others and look directly at him. He shuddered, feeling that familiar chill.

"Be still," he heard her say inside his head.

Rudy staggered back from the door, legs like rubber. In a paradox of panic and fascination he forced himself back to his spy-hole.

"That so, Kneebone?" Rudy heard Manny say before coughing hard once. "Accusing my son of something like this don't sit right." Rudy saw Manny look squarely at Beck. "You know, Beck, we haven't known each other very long, and ever since you been around, things don't sit right either. Now I see you have *your* people in *my* town, and you don't do me the courtesy of letting me know."

"Manny, come on," Beck said. "The Sids are working in everyone's best interest here, so relax. Without them you wouldn't have the merch back. And we wouldn't be gettin' a clear view of what's really been goin' on right under your nose."

"That so?" Manny said.

"That's right," Beck replied.

"Well, you know what I think, Mr. Beck?"

"No, Manny, what do you think?"

"I think this all don't sit right, and your Tweedledum and Tweedledee here, they look 'n' smell more like feds to me. For that matter you got a bit of that stink on you too. What do you think of that? Am I right?"

"What the hell, Manny!" Beck shouted. "We've been doin' business for more than a year now."

Rudy watched as Manny gave a slow nod. "That's right, and finding out anything about your background to make me feel comfortable has been very, very hard to come by. Seems you're a bit of a . . . ghost. Is that how you put it, Albert?"

"That's right, Pop—a ghost."

"Is this how you show us respect?" Beck asked. "Have you forgotten it's our organization who opened doors to some serious players on your behalf? Does that look like something a bunch of low-paid flatfoot feds would do?"

"It might," Manny said, "if the payoff was sweet enough."

Rudy felt the mood in the room drop about ten degrees.

"You know why I have an ulcer, Mr. Beck?" Manny patted the side of his stomach. "My ulcer is like a bad cousin who is unpleasant to have around, but provides good information."

"Oh yeah? So, Manny, what is your . . . ulcer telling you now?"

"It's tellin' me, apart from you enriching the cornfield out back, we have no more business here."

Beck stood abruptly. "Now look, old man, you're pushin' too far!"

"No, you Irish prick, I haven't even begun to push," Manny said.

Sharp exchanges began amongst all the men at the table.

"Time to run, Golliwog—quick quick!" Rudy heard Insidia whisper—but not in his mind this time. It sounded like she was right behind him. "Find a way out—or die with the rest."

Rudy swung around on his heels, back pressed against the door—only to see no one there. Panic gripped him.

"Gotta go, gotta go—now!" he muttered. "Goddess, show me the way."

His eyes darted about the darkened space, then aloft. In this room the roof structure was high and open, exposing heavy rafters above. Some rafters had old meat hooks attached to metal stirrups for hanging things on. Rudy looked back at the floor directly below. Now he knew why the bloodstains were there.

Oh fuck! Oh fuck!

He continued to scan about, stopping finally at the wall opposite. Up high moonlight filtered through gaps in the roughly added vertical boards. At the same time, he heard the tension in the voices that continued to rise out in the boardroom.

That's an old window!

Looking for a way to climb, he moved over to use the table.

"No one threatens me that way, Caracara," Beck shouted from the other room. "No one. We're done!"

"Hurry, Golliwog! Things are about to get nasty," Insidia's voice urged Rudy.

"Shit shit shit!" Rudy muttered.

Teeth gritted, he began to give the table a shove to a position under the boarded window. One of the legs caught the rug underneath and pulled up the end of the rug, exposing the floor underneath.

A single gunshot silenced all the shouting from the main room.

Then, "The bitch shot me!" Manny yelled.

"Sidia! Calm down!" Beck said. "Everyone just calm down."

"Screw that!" Manny said.

Three rapid shots rang out. The sound of furniture being overturned and people diving for cover filled the next seconds.

"No loose ends!" Vince shouted.

All of a sudden, everyone in the room who had a gun began to use it. Rudy could hear shots erupt from every corner of the room. Several rounds passed through the front wall of his small prison, including the door. Some whistled past close enough for Rudy to feel the wind and splinter spray. He hit the deck in panic.

"Typical! Stupid bitch brings a toy and painted nails to a gunfight," Rudy heard Vince say. "This one's yours, bitch!"

"Hey! Careful, you idiot, you almost got me!" Albert yelled.

Goddess, save me! Rudy prayed, eyes shut.

A body hit the wall next to Rudy's door, hard. It slid to the floor and then Rudy heard the person struggling to stand.

"Goddamn it! TAKE 'EM DOWN!" Manny shouted amidst the exchange.

"Better tell your bruisers to back off, Manny," Beck said. "Sidia won't go gentle if she gets pissed."

BANG! BANG! BANG!

"Ha!" Vince shouted. "I got her! I got her! . . . Oh shit."

"Like to try again, sweetheart?" Insidia asked for all to hear. She gave a creepy little laugh. "You'll need more than *that* to end me, I'm afraid, meat-bag."

"Who the fuck are you people?" Manny said. "Someone kill that goddamn whore!"

BANG! BANG! BANG!

"What the? Oh, shit!"

Again the sound of female laughter cut through the din.

More gunshots. Sounds of people scrambling for cover and furniture smashing against the walls made Rudy's jaw clench.

"AHHHH! Fuck! Albert! Come on. Throw me your other piece!"

Bang! Bang! Bang! Bang!

"Not fucking likely, Vince."

More laughter.

"I warned you, Manny—she's coming for you," Beck yelled.

"Will someone *please* KILL THIS BITCH?" Manny roared.

"My pleasure, boss!" came Fritz's voice. "This is for you, peaches."

Bang! Bang!

"LITTLE VINCE! THE OTHER ONE! GET THE OTHER ONE FIRST!" Albert shouted.

BOOM chk-chk BOOM chk-chk BOOM!

Two of the heavy rounds punched fist-sized holes on either side of Rudy's door. The last blew the door lock off and the door swung ajar a couple of inches.

"Problem, boss!" Fritz said. "He blew half her face off—and she still ain't dead!"

"I see that, blockhead!" Vince said. "Blow the other half off, you idiot, and get Pop outta here!

"Look out!"

"Throw me that 12-gauge! C'mere, bitch. I'm gonna open more pretty holes in you than God ever intended."

A sudden quiet fell. Then came a thump and a clatter, like a piece of timber falling to ground.

"You know, pie-face . . ." Insidia said.

Rudy heard briefsounds of a struggle. and then Insidia continued, "I think I'm going to shove this weapon right up your . . ."

Then Rudy heard three crushing body blows, and something heavy crashed against the wall in front of him. A plume of decades-old dust erupted from the point of impact, and then a gurgling groan followed as the body slid to the ground.

"Did that hurt, pie-face. Here, let me help you up. This will be worse."

There was a click-click-click of high-heels crossing the room toward Rudy.

"AHHH! Ahh!"

"Oh, you big baby, Fritz. Try this on for size."

Womp!

"OH Jeeesus . . . She's not gonna . . . Someone get that bitch offa him!"

"Fuck, Manny! She really did shove it up his—"

BOOM chk-chk BOOM!

"Who's next?" Insidia said. "You'll do. Come here, sweetheart. This'll be fun."

"Help! Fuck! My gun!"

"Here, then. Have it back."

Womp!

"Help! Someone shoot this other prick! Arrr, NO you don't! Ahhh! Get off me, you dumb fuck. No no, ahh—AHH!"

"Your soul is mine, meat-sack." That was Insidio's voice.

"Christ! Let me outta here!" Little Vince yelled.

"Sorry," Insidia said. "You can't leave now, boys. Party's just getting started. Beck! Sabastian! Retrieve the package and meet us outside. Insidio! Left!"

"Got it!"

Shump shump shump.

"Errrr gorrr!"

Thud!

At the far end of the murderous space, Rudy heard others burst through the door. Another hail of gunshots, including automatic weapons, rang out. Bullet holes riddled the front wall of Rudy's room as he stayed pinned to the floor under the table.

Bang . . . bang-bang!

"Ahh, I'm hit! Goddamn, I'm gut-shot!"

Bang bang!

"You poor, sad human," Insidio said. "Here, allow me to help with that!"

Shump shump.

Thud.

"Problem solved."

"Johnny, Shultz," Vince yelled. "I'm hit. Take out the one with that fuckin' trench knife before he butchers the rest of us!"

"We all are trying, you moron!" Albert shouted. "GET POP OUTTA HERE, VINCE, GOD DAMN IT!"

Rudy heard a short, grisly scream and then the sound of something bouncing on the floor twice and rolling a short distance.

"Christ! He just cut Johnny's friggin head off with that thing."

"Well, kill the prick properly, numb-nuts, so he doesn't do it again!" Vince shouted.

"Come here, you!

Bang-bang—click-click.

"Ah! Gun's jammed!"

"Al! Behind you!" Vince shouted.

Rudy heard fumbling and a short struggle, then the clatter of something heavy hitting the floor and sliding. A brutal slap followed, as if someone delivered a cruel backhand.

"Now it's personal, you demon bitch," Vince said. "I'm gonna stomp you good!"

"At least you are observant, meat-sack, so come see what Mama has for you," Rudy heard Insidia say.

Three running steps followed, and then a shriek like nothing living on this world shattered everyone's ears. Gunshots and mayhem rained down on everyone a moment after.

"Fuck, did you see that?" someone cried. "We're all gonna die."

Another body struck the front wall of Rudy's room and three shump shump shump thrusts were heard.

"Correct," Rudy heard Insidio say. "Walter, where are you going? Get back here!"

Shump.

A final cough and gurgle, and then the sound of another thudding fall made Rudy cringe.

"We'll see to him shortly," Insidia said. "Mop that one up, would you."

Near hysteria Rudy's eyes fell on a square outline cut into the floor, previously covered by the rug. Another hail of gunshots forced Rudy to stay low. Close to his reach he saw a rusty bolt-and-plate latch screwed into the square.

A lock! Locks keep things closed.

As he reached for the bolt, a storm of curses, furious obscenities, and fearful shouts rang out, marking another brutal struggle. Rudy tried to wiggle the bolt across to unlock it. It was stiff and hard to budge.

"Come on, move, dammit!"

Pushing hard on the stubborn bolt, Rudy felt his hand slip and get cut, which caused him to reel.

"Ahhh! God . . . ahh!"

Enduring the cut as best he could, he grabbed the bolt again. Using all his strength, he worked the bolt back and forth to where it finally snapped back. Amidst the boom-crack of many firearms, demonic shrieks, and men being ferociously executed, Rudy hauled up the trapdoor and peered down. Below he saw a narrow staircase, one recently used as evidenced by the bloody boot print he could see on the dusty top step leading down into the darkness.

Who else is down there?

"Hurry, Golliwog," he heard Insidia say next to his right ear. "Death is looking for you!"

Fear of who might be waiting below felt almost welcoming compared to the evil closing in. Taking a breath, Rudy plunged down into the darkness. The trapdoor slammed shut.

CHAPTER

5

Terror and Deception

Trembling, Rudy felt his way down the steep stairway into the cold and stale air of the chamber below. Behind him at the top of the stairs, he heard the slap-crack of the trapdoor being locked. Standing partway down the steps, in the pitch black and with one hand on a wall that felt like cold stone, he snapped a look back up in the direction of the sound.

Trapped.

Trembling, he stepped down to flee—but tripped. Rudy fell down the last stairs in a horror roll of shoulders, elbows, ribs, and shins. He finished with a thud in a heap at the bottom. For a moment, semiconscious with face still flat against the cold stone floor, he lay there in the darkness. With a thundering headache from the fall, he stirred, pushing himself up to a sitting position. He reached out to get his bearings and his hand met a wall. Random shots and screams pointed the way back up. He felt around and found the bottom step. Then, tracing the edge, he felt the corner of the stone wall, or was it brick? Cautiously he pushed to a standing position, and feeling along the wall surface, his fingers found a light switch.

Click.

Reluctantly a single dusty florescent tube blinked to life, revealing an unkempt, dank cellar. Rudy saw some shelves and covered articles on the right, dusty wine cases and packing boxes on the left. He looked about warily.

No one here.

With his panic eased, he looked about for a weapon. Something that might be able to be swung or used to stab anyone or anything that moved.

Nothing!

Then his eyes widened. In the shadows at the far end to the left, he saw another door.

A way out! Oh, Goddess, let it be a way out.

He rushed to it and tried the handle.

Locked!

He struggled, trying to force the door open with his shoulder.

"Come on, damn it."

Then he spotted a ring of long-shafted keys hanging from a hook on a board by the door. Grabbing them, he inserted the first key into the lock. No good. The second turned easily, one of the sweetest sounds he'd remember for the rest of his life. The door opened outward into a well-lit tunnel. Festoon lights hung along the left wall all the way to the other end, where a stairway leading up could be seen. Praying it was his escape, Rudy ran forward, remembering the stories told at the depot about old Prohibition tunnels like this.

"Never thought they were true," he mumbled.

Rudy moved toward the way up as fast as his legs would carry him. Sudden banging noises from the cellar behind him set his pulse racing again. Looking over his shoulder in terror once more, he barely touched the bottom step before bolting up the stairs. At the top was a rusty metal hatch. Cautiously he pressed upward. The hinges made a dry, metal-on-metal squeal as the hatch came to rest against another metal obstacle. Rudy climbed out of the tunnel, remaining in a crouched position behind a storage container. Looking about, he tried to get his bearings. He could see the tannery's main building where all the horror had taken place. Then he heard voices.

"You go left, Sabastian." That was Beck. "The spade's got to be here somewhere. She wants him alive."

Desperately Rudy looked for a way out. The rear perimeter fence ran only a few paces from where he crouched. There in front of him, a small security gate offered freedom. Then he saw the chain and heavy padlock, dashing all hope of escape. He heard the crunch of gravel underfoot.

One of them's close. "Goddess, I need a way out," he muttered.

He scurried to the end of his cover. From there his eye line followed the broadside of the main building to the front where they had entered. To the left he saw his cab.

Run!

***

The tortured screams inside the tannery suddenly gave way to an eerie silence with the crack of two final gunshots. Outside the tannery office entrance, the clouds were thinning, though a light rain still fell. Translucent sheets of mist rolled eerily about the compound. The office door creaked open, and out into the night stepped an unruffled Insidio and Insidia.

"Did you get it"? Insidio asked.

Insidia pulled an onyx disc from her pocket and showed it to Insidio. "The old man had it in his jacket pocket next to his heart. . . . I took them both."

"Good. Now we can complete what we started."

"What about Kneebone?"

Insidio shrugged. "Escaped. No great harm. Exited the moment you started the fun."

They both looked about the compound. Insidia pointed to the perimeter of the grounds in the east.

"There, struggling to go through the fence," she said.

"He's out of range," said Insidio.

"Never mind. We now have a better alternative. Rudy Barabbas will do just fine."

Insidio shook his head. "You know you can't use him. His karma is too high in the positive. They will be watching."

"If we can convert him, he will sustain us indefinitely here and have many uses. He only has to agree once."

"And if he doesn't?"

"Then I will be most put out, and Rudy Barabbas very regretful of his circumstance. But I like a challenge. I sense my Golliwog should be emerging." She looked around the compound. "Right about . . . now."

Squelching steps were heard pounding through mud and wet grass in their direction along the side of the building.

Still beyond their point of view and oblivious to how close they were, Rudy's focus was on escaping from Beck and Sabastian closing in from behind. Rudy charged toward the front of the building, intent on stopping for no one. He misjudged the height of a dilapidated low fence at the building's corner and went sprawling facedown in the mud. Scrambling to his knees, he looked up and saw his cab. Sprinting to it, unaware he was being watched, he reached out for the door handle and attempted to jerk it open. It wouldn't budge. Holding the door handle with one hand, he placed a foot on the car to pull harder.

"No. No no! Goddamn you, come on, open!"

From his right he felt a presence and stopped. Turning slowly with dread, he saw Insidia and Insidio watching from the veranda. He thought he heard them laughing. Frantically he struggled with the door again.

"Keys, keys, keys." Hands shaking, he dug into his pocket and extracted the keys. Inserting it into the lock, he turned it and pulled on the door again. This time it moved.

"Yes!"

Just as he swung the door wide, all time-space activity inside the tannery perimeter stopped, including Rudy, who froze in place. Only Insidia and Insidio remained animated.

"You know," Insidia said. "I feel refreshed after the drinking of those souls inside." Hungrily she eyed the frozen figure of Rudy. "I think we *should* take the chance and consume him anyway. Rudy Barabbas has a vast reserve of positive karma. If we blended both his and Walter's soul cores, the karmic potential could sustain us long enough to take over this prison world. We could set up an independent life-stream generator of our own."

"No," said Insidio. "*She* wouldn't agree to that at all. Such an action would be in direct violation of Citadel Council Law One: *'No sentient life may be removed from the Superverse karmic register without unanimous sanction of all Citadel Council members. All sentient life has the right to independent life streams. Choice through free will in an environment of random evolution is mandatory.'* It's an offense worthy of being banished to the Echaa Realms for erasure."

"We've faced worse," Insidia said.

"No, we haven't. A sentence there would be final if we were caught and convicted. Nothing comes back from the Echaa Realms. Doing the right thing by one such as Rudy Barabbas could prove to be to our advantage one day."

"So I guess using him as a travel snack is out of the question now."

"Be serious, Insidia. We need to consider this carefully. Don't want to be pushed over the edge for something trivial."

Insidia sighed. "Being shackled by the Lord of Chaos is beneath us. I am weary of doing Evercycle Three's bidding. Lord of Chaos or not, I will be free of her."

Insidio gave a nod and asked, "Where are Beck and Sabastian?"

They both looked to the side of the building as if expecting their two subordinates to emerge.

"Hm, that is strange," Insidia said.

Insidio looked skyward, saying, "Stay your hand, for now. She approaches."

Suddenly both Insidia and Insidio's physical forms became translucent, and they merged to form one hideous Ultra Demon. A fine line divided the demon's merged figure down the center, identifying their convergence. Several feet away a silver shaft of light struck the ground with the sound of swirling broken glass. When it dissipated, the curvaceous figure of a woman in a Venetian maiden's dress stood in its place. She had a head of long auburn hair and wild sapphire eyes. She stood for a moment looking about, paying particular attention to Rudy.

"Well, it seems I've come a tad overdressed," she muttered to herself.

She ran her fingers down her sternum as if undoing a zipper. Her attire morphed a fraction later to a stylish pantsuit more befitting of the Earth period.

Her feet, however, were still covered by gold Venetian sandals, totally out of place. Curiously no mud or slop from the earlier rain appeared to touch her feet.

A sneer crossed her expression, which soured the beauty of her face. "This world smells and feels the same every time." She approached the demon on the veranda with confident strides, glaring straight at it. "Insidius," she said, addressing her servant. "The departure of many unsanctioned soul cores from this timeline just lit up the Karmic Administration register worse than an exploding star system. I ordered this operation be covert. Unseen *in*, unseen *out*."

Insidius drifted back half a foot. "We apologize, Evercycle Three, but there was no alternative. The one called Rudy Barabbas was about to be removed from this timeline by one or more of our charges for reasons of their own. We had to intervene. Things unpredictably escalated. We had to ensure no witnesses."

"Where have you sent all the soul cores?"

"They are contained within our personal domain. None will discover them there."

"But they will send someone to investigate the absences here, you fool."

"Regrettably, yes, my lady, but we felt this option still conformed to your instructions."

Evercycle Three stood there sullen for a moment, thinking. "Very well. You will see *that* individual"—she pointed to Rudy—"remains unharmed until I deem otherwise. He is supposed to be in your custody. His positive personal karma is not yours to consume. Is that clear?"

"Yes, my lady."

Evercycle Three suddenly paused in her train of thought. "I could have sworn for a moment . . . I felt a warden's presence."

"We feel no one," Insidius said.

"Of course you don't. That requires subtlety."

With nothing tangible detected, Three shook her head and dismissed the notion, then focused back on the demon.

"Remember, Insidius, regardless of whatever scheme for power and independence you contemplate, know I feel every thread your evil genius concocts. Do not seek to outflank me. I will not hesitate to send you to the Echaa Realms for erasure in a blink."

"We sincerely apologize, my lady. We have not been able to feed on the souls of the lost for so long, and that depletes our strength and focus in this world. The one called Kneebone has scant reserves left for us to make use of. Rudy Barabbas could sustain us beyond our realm for a considerable time."

Three eyed the demon. "You heard my order, Insidius. Were you not the only Ultra Demon strong enough to withstand the debilitating effects of mortal-side karmic radiation, I would have had you erased long ago. Now do your job. I want Rudy Barabbas tethered and found by Zero's agents. Ensure he encounters Warden Bloch. He will arrive soon. Their destinies must collide. I'll do the rest. Their actions here on Earth and later on Planet Tora will shift the time-space axis of the entire intercosmos to my advantage. Everything will be reset to the balance intended before the Great Event. Then, the one who should rightfully be in charge of existence will be me. Lord Zero and the rest of the council will have no choice but to do *my* bidding, and the reins of existence will be mine."

"We are yours to command, Lord of Chaos. But we cannot sustain our hold on this plane of existence without a viable donor. May we consume a small token of the human Rudy Barabbas's soul core so we may complete our mission?"

A cold stare met their request as Evercycle Three contemplated the ramifications. "Very well. But only as much as it takes to activate the tether already in place, no more. Use what's left of Kneebone completely if necessary. Send what remains on to the Echaa Realms for erasure. I will see it sanctioned." Three looked to the building behind Insidius. "The human called Vince in there —that one is useful to me. His soul core was the only one I was able to intercept before you harvested everyone inside. I have resurrected him. Keep him here to serve my purpose. He is now part of *my* retinue. Intelligence has been provided strongly suggesting that Lord Zero needs to recover a witness sent to this world from Tora. They are to testify against my son, Herrex, for additional crimes against existence. Allow Commander Bloch to lead you to them. I want that witness. Intercept them before they are in the custody of Lord Zero's agents." She looked over to Rudy. "Keep that one close, and unharmed. You understand me, Insidius? Unharmed."

"We will do as you order."

"Do not fail me, Insidius."

Three cast her view skyward and lifted her arms. Both she and Insidius vaporized from sight, and the local time-space Continuum resumed.

Rudy lurched and fell forward, catching himself on the side of the cab with one hand. He looked about with wide eyes. With no threat to be seen, he hastily climbed inside the cab. In the distance he saw Kneebone trying to scramble through a hole in the fence. His jacket snagged on some wire, and he struggled to break free before disappearing into the shadows.

With the door still wide open Rudy started the engine and stamped on the gas, yanking the door shut as he did so. The cab's wheels spun and the vehicle surged forward. Rudy swung the cab around and pointed it at the gates, his head swiveling left and right for the two evils who had stood on the veranda. At full throttle Rudy pushed the cab toward freedom for all it was worth. It burst through the closed gates, away from the horrors of the tannery and toward the lights of town in the distance.

✳✳✳

A mile down the road Rudy eased off the accelerator and took in a large breath. "Ain't no one ever goin' catch Rudy Barabbas like that again . . . ever."

Then, from the backseat, a translucent hand reached over and slid long, gnarled, chilling fingers around the back of Rudy's neck.

"AHHHH! AHHH!"

In horror Rudy looked into his rearview mirror to see the hideous features of something that vaguely resembled Insidia and Insidio—almost like they'd joined together in one being now.

"Almost, Golliwog. Time to pay your debt!" The voice confirmed Rudy's guess that this was *both* Insidia and Insidio.

Suddenly a potent unseen force struck the side of the cab hard enough to shove it across the road. Its nose plowed into a ditch, causing the vehicle to flip and roll several times.

Rudy felt the world spin, with shattering glass and crushing metal encapsulating him before everything fell into darkness.

ACT 2

CHAPTER

6

Second Chance

Sometime later . . .

Rudy felt pain throughout his entire being. Taking in a sharp breath through his nostrils, he could smell dust and debris mixed with gasoline. The echo of a voice began to stir in his mind like some faraway calling.

"Rudy? Rudy, can you hear me? Follow my voice Rudy. Move toward my voice."

Becoming aware he was on the ground facedown in a sprawl, Rudy attempted to move an arm. Pain through his shoulder speared him as certain as if he'd been skewered with a blade. He moved a leg, and in his lower back a feeling of molten lead being poured into the base of his spine shocked him into full consciousness. He tried to sit up. The pain took his breath away.

"Take it easy, Rudy," came the sympathetic, but unfamiliar voice of a woman. "You are in shock, and we don't have much time. You have been through quite an ordeal, but you are safe now. Move slowly. Your body has been damaged. Several bones are broken."

Her voice did not sound threatening; if anything it was comforting. Face covered in mud, Rudy lifted his head in the direction of the voice and attempted to focus on who was speaking. Pain shocked its way down his spine again. Slowly Rudy could see the figure of a dog backlit by the headlights of the destroyed cab now on its side. There was no one else to be seen. He strained to look around.

"Everything will be alright, Rudy," she said, making Rudy turn all his focus on the dog.

"Shock . . . you're in shock," he told himself. "Dogs don't talk."

"The demon has gone, for now. I'm sorry, but this was the only way I could save you."

Rudy looked past the dog, desperately hoping to see a woman speaking, but there was only the bent wreck of the cab. Not knowing what to think, Rudy rolled onto his back, with pain from many parts of his body pressing him to stop moving. He closed his eyes again and took some breaths to try to steady his throbbing head.

"I'll make everything clear to you later, Rudy. Right now I need to move you from this place to keep you safe. Those who held you captive will return to look for you the moment they have regenerated. You are going to go to sleep for a little while now, Rudy. Rest, and we'll speak again soon, I promise."

With the end of those words, like a swirling dream, Rudy fell back into unconsciousness with the silhouette of the mysterious talking dog fading as the last fixed point in his mind.

***

The next thing Rudy knew, he was waking to the smell of cigarette smoke and old furniture. Then his attention went to the absence of the horrendous pain he'd felt at the crash site, aside from a few lingering aches. He could feel that wherever he was, it wasn't a large space by any means. He felt someone pull the corner of a blanket up over his shoulder.

"He gonna be alright?" asked the gentle voice of an old woman.

"Yes, Kate, he'll be fine," said the same female voice from the crash site.

"He has a big part to play in all this now."

Rudy moved and the warm padded surface he was lying on creaked a little. The pillow supporting his face felt warm and comforting. As his eyes blinked open, he found the light in the room to be soft, almost yellow. He could hear thunder and rain in the background. Cigarette smoke tickled his nose again. His blurred vision took a few seconds to focus, but when it did, what surrounded him took him by surprise. Wherever he was, he was lying on someone's couch in the sitting room of a modest apartment. A black-and-white television sat over in one corner, turned on with the sound very low. A Danny Kaye movie he'd seen before was playing. A dark-wood cabinet stood against the left wall adjacent to the TV. One shelf held small, framed black-and-white photos of families and uniformed men of a bygone era. The place had the cozy feel and the scents of being lived in for some time. Opposite Rudy sat an older African-American woman in an easy chair. She had neck-length dark hair framing a kind face, and she was wearing a green housedress.

"He's stirrin'," the woman said, looking at him. "You want me to make coffee? Or should he have somethin' stronger?"

"Coffee will be fine, thank you, Kate. I need him thinking straight for what he needs to hear."

Rudy realized that the female with the voice from the car accident stood or sat very close to his head, but out of view. He watched the one named Kate stand. She seemed to have some trouble with her hip by the way she placed her hand on it. She looked at him with a frown.

"I'll make it doubly strong, just to make sure he knows he's not dreamin' after you take his brain into the twilight zone and back."

Kate walked past the foot of Rudy's bed. She gave him a gentle smile and left the warm room through a doorway. When she flicked on the light in the next room, Rudy caught a glimpse of green kitchen cupboards suspended on one wall. Noises of running water and the clink of cups signaled activity.

"So … time we had a chat, then," said that same female voice.

He heard the sound of something drop onto the floor behind him. Then, trotting around into plain view, came that same dog he'd been seeing all night: a medium-sized canine with short gray fur and a black patch over her left eye. The tip was missing off her right ear too. She stood there in front of him, almost face to snout. Looking at him, her tail had the tiniest wag, and she wore an expression, as far as dogs go, as if she were smiling. She smelled kind of like roses—not like a dog at all, his nose told him. Her breed was a little confusing at first. Then a flicker of memory had him recall a dog belonging to his Australian English teacher back in Jamaica. *Blue* they'd called her, on account of her being a blue heeler.

The two stared at each other for a long moment.

"Well, you don't look too much the worse for wear," the dog said.

Rudy's mouth fell open in amazement. She had spoken to him in the clearest educated English tone, just like one of those classy English actresses he'd seen in films. Rudy pressed himself up on his elbows, jaw still dropped.

"Close your mouth before you catch something unsavory," the dog said. "Now, before you get all bamboozled about what you are or aren't seeing and hearing, yes, I am a dog—well, at the moment anyway. Yes, I'm talking, and no, you are not hallucinating. You can call me 'Dogg.' That's spelled with two G's, so there is no confusion. I am a warden profiler for the Citadel Council. I answer to Evercycle Zero, Lord of Life's Spark, one of the oldest creators of existence."

"Uhhh … one of … one of the oldest?"

"Yes, there are nine others. The Citadel Council is responsible for the stability and evolution of existence. Your life cycle flagged some interest with one of their administrative bodies, the Karma Re-Evolution Division. I've been assigned to look into your case and act as your guardian until certain issues are rectified."

Rudy sat there, still wearing a stunned expression. It was clear he was thinking, but about what exactly, Dogg couldn't tell.

"Rudy. It's all true, I promise you. Nod and tell me you heard all that."

Rudy nodded, mouth still open and having an expression like he'd been slapped with a wet fish.

"Coffee," Kate said as she appeared from the kitchen with mug in hand.

Rudy accepted the offered mug with a nod of thanks, and then watched Kate look to Dogg with a smile.

"You sure he's takin' all that in?" Kate asked.

Rudy shifted himself to a sitting position, still feeling a little sore.

"Yes, I'm sure," said Dogg. "He's just taking a little time to process things. Isn't that right, Rudy?"

Rudy's eyes flicked from one to the other.

"Drink up, son," Kate said. "There's a lot more o' that comin' your way." She moved to sit down in her easy chair.

Dogg paid her a glance before refocusing on Rudy. "Her name is really Katheryn Hepburn, like the actress, but with the first name spelled differently," Dogg said. "And she prefers 'Kate.' She will see to your basic needs while you are here. You can trust her; she's one of my best."

"What … What, umm …" Rudy's words stalled, and he cleared his throat. "Umm. What ha … What ha—"

"What happened to you?" Dogg interrupted. "You were being hunted by the infamous serial killer, Walter Kneebone, a ruthless monster of a human being who wanted you to be his replacement. Then you were hijacked by his employer, an Ultra Demon called Insidius."

Rudy blinked and focused on Dogg. None of this made any sense—at all. "Replacement? Replacement for what?" Rudy said, the words barely squeezing from his lips. "I thought they wanted the delivery I was carrying."

"Oh, Rudy, they wanted a lot more from you than that. They wanted your living essence. Walter Kneebone's soul belongs to Insidius too. Insidius is neither Spector nor even Arch Demon. Insidius is specifically an Ultra Dark Hoarier Demon whose interests align with Evercycle Three, Lord of Chaos. Spectacularly nasty in anyone's world or any realm they gain access to. Two of the individuals inside the tannery you encountered, Beck and Sabastian, were also in Insidius's employ."

Rudy let out a slow breath, still not sure where all this was going. "I thought Hell had swallowed me up."

"In a sense, it had," Dogg said. "The realms of Heaven and Hell surround your race in equal parts at all times, and there are many things in between. It's your free will that feeds one or the other's strength."

Now Rudy nodded. "Goddess saved me."

Dogg looked at him for a moment. "Yes, you might say she's part of that. But your good karma protected you—this time. With every soul core's rebirth on your world, they bring with them a little something special. *You*, Rudy Barabbas, were born with what we like to call 'uncanny luck.' It's why you managed to slip away from your pursuers unaware of the peril you were in. Something that for others in the same circumstance would have most likely been their end."

Rudy raised his eyebrows. "Huh? What do you mean?"

"The moment your head popped up from under that building, Beck and Sabastian were waiting for you. They all but had you too, but missed their chance when you ran and fell over that fence out of reach. In that moment they encountered me. I depleted my greater soul-core reserves dealing with them quietly. Couldn't get to you in time."

Rudy blew a breath of relief through fluttering lips. "Me old mom always said I had a little angel watchin' over me."

"Yes. That attribute *is*, I believe, partly to do with why you are so important to our enemies. Insidius knows if you could be turned or manipulated to do their bidding, just as Walter Kneebone has, then some of your luck will go their way. I think they also intend to use you as an unwitting spy, something *we* can use to our advantage."

"Spy …" said Rudy, then sighed. "Hey, I drive cabs for a living. I'm no James Bond. I just want to make a good life for me and Mala, who would skin me alive if she knew what I've been up to."

Here Kate chuckled. "Woman sounds sensible to me," she said. "Least *she* won't damn you to the Hell Realms like Insidius would."

"Listen. I never saw them before tonight, right."

Dogg sat down, and her voice softened. "Yes, Rudy, we know."

"All I want is to be as far from them as possible."

Dog gave a single nod. "Yes, Rudy, we know. However, that will prove difficult until we sort matters out, I'm afraid. Once Insidius has a target, they are relentless in acquiring it. They can't be killed, don't sleep, and have absolutely no compassion in the methods they employ to achieve that goal."

Rudy felt his heart jump. "So what are you saying—my life is over?"

"As you know it, yes."

Rudy's eyes went wide and he shook his head.

"When you fled to your vehicle attempting to escape the horrors going on inside the tannery," Dogg said, "the timeline was temporarily frozen by another even greater being. Insidius's employer, Evercycle Three, I suspect. Three arrived and placed a time-space cavion blind over the tannery to communicate with Insidius uninterrupted. All the markers left behind suggest as much."

Closing his eyes, Rudy took a sip of coffee and then rubbed his face with his free hand.

"Told you his brain would hurt," Kate said.

"A cavion what? And . . . why?" Rudy asked.

"Why exactly, I'm yet to establish," Dogg said. "But it directly concerned you to some degree, I know that much. Otherwise you would have been just another loose end to them. They would have dealt with you on the spot. Being inside the cavion perimeter undetected at the time, I too was frozen for a short while. But some weakness occurred in the cavion field long enough to release me before I was discovered. That is why I was helpless to aid you until later."

"Wow. It all seems like a shifting bad dream in me head now," Rudy said.

"I know all this is beyond your fathoming," Dogg went on. "But if it helps, Evercycles like Three are galaxies stronger than the likes of Insidius."

"Oh, gee, great to know," Rudy said.

"No mortal is meant to remember anything during the time a being such as Evercycle Three deigns to set foot on your world."

"Has she been here before?" Rudy asked.

"Yes, many times. Not being mortal like you, the cavion field does not affect me. As a result I remember most of what occurs. But I really need your help now and maybe a little of that luck you carry will rub off on all of us too."

"No way, mon. All *I* need to do is go home and get ready to go back to Jamaica, where I belong," Rudy said. "This place has been nothing but trouble ever since I arrived."

His mind made up, Rudy set his mug down on the floor and swung his feet off the couch, attempting to stand.

"No, Rudy," said Dogg flatly. Her words stalled his intention. "I am afraid that will never be possible, ever again."

Rudy slumped back into the couch, and his face fell as the impact of Dogg's words annihilated his dreams of a new life with his Mala.

"Insidius will be counting on you returning to your apartment. *This* is your home now. Unless you want to be taken—again."

Rudy shook his head and looked at Kate.

"You better listen to her," Kate said. "She knows what she's talkin' about."

Rudy paused, thinking. Finally he shrugged. "Okay, I'll help. Not like I have a real choice, do I? What do you want me to do?"

Dogg stood up. "Excellent! I managed to banish Insidius for possibly thirty-six hours."

"Possibly? Really?" Rudy said. "That's the best you got?"

"One of our agents and their team are coming here to find someone very important to the stability of all existence. We have twenty-four hours."

"But you just said thirty-six hours."

"We have only *twenty-four* hours to arrange for you to meet them. They will need your help. Far from your world, there has been a great war. A key witness to the heinous crimes committed has been hidden on your world. We must do what we can to aid the team to find that witness before Insidius does. My plan is to expose *you* just long enough for Insidius to come sniffing about and remain distracted."

Rudy stared at Dogg for a moment, then said, "Uhhhh . . . Is there a Plan B?"

"No. We must keep them chasing shadows 'til our agents can sort the mess out. Don't worry, though: Insidius won't hurt you while they think you're useful."

Rudy began to straighten up, pursing his lips as he felt butterflies in his stomach. "Define *hurt*."

"Like I said, don't worry, Rudy," Dogg continued. "I'll be very close by, I promise. I won't let anything happen to you. Insidius thinks you have been tethered from when they grabbed you in the cab. One of the Insidius personalities must have touched you to implant the tether."

Rudy began to examine his arms and legs as Dogg went on.

"You may have felt the tiniest cold tickle when they did it. It's a kind of . . . a bug that demons use to keep track of their subordinates. It allows them to hear and see what's happening around you, amongst other things. I disabled your tether from your thigh while you were unconscious."

Rudy thought hard and vaguely remembered the feeling of Insidia's hand on his thigh in the cab and how her cold touch had unnerved him. He rubbed his right leg.

"Yep, that's the one," said Dogg.

Rudy swallowed. "You got it out, right?"

"No, I'm sorry. To remove it here would cause you great pain and permanent disability. Don't worry. It's quite harmless now. I took control of its function at the crash site before I brought you here. I can turn it on and off at will. Now we can use it against them."

"How does that help?" asked Rudy while looking at his thigh.

"By feeding them false information. Using their tether against them, we can keep Insidius running in circles 'til we find the one everyone is searching for. Now take your cab keys on the sideboard there. I need you to go back to the depot. It's only a couple blocks from here. Hand them in for the end of shift just like nothing happened."

Dogg pointed her nose toward the sideboard next to a doorway leading into a hallway exit.

Rudy frowned. "But me cab is scrap and hours have passed. The boss is gonna have me hide for that."

"Don't worry about that, Rudy," Dogg said. "Everything will work out fine. You must now go about your business as if everything is quite ordinary. When you do encounter the agents I mentioned, you mustn't tell them you are working for me—for now."

"Huh? Why? Aren't we all on the same side?"

"Yes, we are, but knowing your involvement as far as I do, we can't take the chance of skewing this timeline any further."

"Sounds odd to me," Rudy said. "Wouldn't them knowing I'm part of your team hel—"

"Please, Rudy. There are security issues here. Just do as I ask. I'll tell them everything when the time is right, and I'll have your back in the meantime. How are your bones now? Any aches or pains?"

Rudy felt his arms and torso where only a short while ago he'd been in severe pain. "Well, I feel a little strange, but nothing hurts anymore."

"You'll be able to make the walk back to base with no trouble, then. When that's done, come straight back here to await further orders and Kate will have a meal ready for you."

Rudy stood and now noticed that he was in a complete fresh change of clothes. His open leather jacket revealed a brand-new dark wool jumper underneath. Even his denims and Converse Union high-tops were spotless.

"Whoa, mon. How did you change my—"

"Didn't think it fair to leave you in the sorry state you were in when we brought you back. Kate made sure everything was clean and tidy. Even got you that George Gervin San Antonio Spurs shirt you've been wanting so much. You'll also find two tickets in your pocket for the next Spurs game at the Hemisfair Arena."

Rudy pulled at the front of his jumper to see the new shirt against his skin. "How the . . . ?" Rudy looked up, brain spinning. " How could you even know? Um . . ." He grinned at both of them. "Thank you."

"Call it perks of the job I have in mind for you, if you wouldn't mind helping us out," Dogg said.

"Perks? The whole thing is more like a miracle. Never thought I'd walk straight again. You fixed me body *and* changed me clothes."

"I also fixed that bad knee you were using before the accident as well. Didn't seem right to leave a loose end. Just call it a little bit of magic." Dogg wagged her tail. "Welcome aboard, then. See you when you get back. Oh, one last thing. To protect us all, while you were asleep, I also suppressed a few of your more . . . umm . . . difficult memories. It will prevent any unnecessary anxiety impeding your judgment in future missions. If you encounter Insidius again, your recollections will be distant, vague. We'll tend to the memories more efficiently when we are in a position with better facilities. There we can also fully remove the tether."

Rudy looked at both of his newfound friends curiously and nodded. "Uh, thanks . . . I think."

He gave a little smile and then proceeded to the door, collecting the keys on his way out.

CHAPTER

7

A Different Life

As Rudy exited the old four-story apartment building where Kate lived, he stepped out into a bleak wet and shadowy cityscape. It was still bitterly cold on his face, but his new clothes shielded him from the chilling fingers of the city's winter. He quickly recognized the surrounding streets of the east side and kept to the shadows as much as possible. Heading back to the depot as ordered, he had no idea how he was going to explain what happened to his cab. Looking at his watch, he stopped in his tracks.

"That can't be right, mon. It should have been hours since me shift finished."

His watch still seemed to be working fine, but it showed the time as 12:50. He squinted at the tiny date window.

"*Saturday?* Is this the same night? No. That can't be right. There's no way that all happened in an hour and a bit. How long was I out?"

Then, from behind, he heard the rumble of a bus coming down the road. He turned and saw it was the number four, heading to the west side—the same bus he caught home most nights after shift. Then he realized this would be just about where it should be if he was riding that bus home. His legs started stepping forward toward Caesar's depot as though someone else had given an order. As he strode along, he checked over his shoulder now and then. He felt as though at any moment he expected to be confronted by someone sinister from a blind alley.

He started thinking on the happenings earlier at the tannery. Just as Dogg had said, his memories of events seemed further away somehow. A bit like one of those early-morning dreams. You know the kind: crystal clear on waking, but by the time you've reached the bathroom, it's melting away like random snowflakes on the ground.

It took him another ten minutes to reach the street where the depot was located. Numerous vehicles had been parked against the curb for the night. Bumper to bumper, their shadows and streetlight reflections made them appear like large river stones on the side of a waterway. As he passed the front of a battered blue Cadillac, a cat bolted from under the front wheels. Heading for a nearby alley, it scrambled over the top of two garbage bins, knocking one over making a hell of a din.

Rudy jumped sideways. "Fuck! Dammit! Bloody animal."

He quickened his pace, eager to distance himself from the calamity.

Did anyone hear?

In the short distance he saw the familiar sign for Caesar's Cabs and breathed a sigh of relief. He could see some cabs parked out front and felt for the keys in his pocket.

How am I gonna to explain the wreck to me boss?

As he went to cross the street that led past the side of the building, he checked right for any surprise traffic. There, parked back in the shadows, sat another cab, one he was all too familiar with. But last he remembered, it had been a torn cluster of steel and collapsed panels.

"What the . . . ?" he whispered.

In the next breath he saw light a flicker on from a ground-floor window adjacent to the cab. Though the light through the curtains was soft, he could see his cab looked quite pristine. It was as though it had been sent to a detailer to make everything shine like new. He stood there dumfounded for a moment, and then, walking forward, he reached out to touch the hood to see if his mind wasn't playing tricks. An inexplicable rise of excitement filled him. Something had finally gone his way. He looked skyward.

"Thank you, Goddess."

With a wide grin he moved to the driver's side door, unlocked it, and climbed in. Inside, he found everything was not just clean, it was showroom new. Even the stale carpet smell that always lingered was gone. He inserted the key into the ignition and gave it a turn. The engine fired up straightaway with a much livelier note than he remembered.

"How did she do all this?"

Feeling more confident about the things he'd been told back at Kate's apartment, Rudy put the cab into drive. He pressed the gas pedal and set off just as Dogg had instructed.

✱✱✱

Moments later Rudy pulled to a stop in the depot's driveway and saw the portly form of his supervisor marching directly toward him from the office. He had that hate-the-world look on his face he always carried—only worse, like someone had kicked one of his shins good and proper. He reminded Rudy of that character Archie Bunker, from the TV series *All in the Family*. Like Archie this guy was the world's most blissfully ignorant bigot. As it happened, *his* name was Archie as well. Rudy stepped out of the cab to meet him.

"Barabbas," Archie barked in his usual punch-in-the-face tone.

Before Rudy could respond, Archie's determined strides faltered as his focus was drawn more and more to Rudy's immaculate vehicle. He stopped, apparently stuck trying to mentally process what he was looking at.

"Goddamn it, what is it about . . . uh, being on time that you . . . um, don't get . . ."

Archie diverted his path and moved to the driver's side, stopping just as his second attempt at a comment ground to a halt as well, and then he glared back at Rudy.

"What the hell have you done to my cab? And where the *hell* have you been?"

"I, uh, well, it got real busy after you called, boss, and so I—"

"Yeah yeah, I heard all about that."

"And then I thought I should clean the cab up to show me sincerity." Now Rudy's words stalled. "Wait—You, um, you heard? What did you hear?"

Archie looked in through the driver's side window, placing his hand on the glass to shield the reflection. "Cleaned it up! Looks more like you had it in the shop for complete rebuild. How did you . . . ?" Archie shook his head. "Never seen it look this good. You did good, kid, real good."

Rudy had never heard Archie be nice to him—ever—and his manner started to make Rudy feel uneasy.

"Oh," Archie said, "I got a call about what you did earlier."

"You . . . did? Uh, and what did I do, apart from cleaning up the cab, I mean?"

Archie stepped back from the vehicle and attempted a smile—it made him look more in pain than happy. "Yep, call came in from one of those City Council suits you drove across town tonight. A Mr. Kneebone."

Rudy felt a cold shiver run up his spine. *Surely Archie read today's paper.*

"Says after what you did for him and his colleagues, he'd like to be reacquainted again real soon."

Another shiver as Rudy thought, *I hope not.*

"Said after the service you provided, he's booked you for the next three days—at top rate, the whole shift! What do you think about that?"

"Uh . . . just doing me job, boss," said Rudy, swallowing. "He really said all that?"

"He sure did. Spoke to him myself. Well, he asked for me in point of fact. To make sure the message got through. Said he'd put in a good word to the council when it comes to the next transport tender. Don't know what you did, Barabbas, but you reeled us in a damn big fish."

"Shark is more like," Rudy muttered.

"What was that?"

"Oh, nothin' at all, boss."

Now Rudy noticed his shift opposite, Herb, emerge from the lunchroom in his usual rough and unshaven way, and head toward the cab. He strode past Rudy with his hand out as if he owned the joint.

"Keys," Herb said.

Rudy tossed them to him by reflex. "Any chance of a lift back?" Rudy asked.

"I'm late," said Herb, catching the keys without missing a step.

"Herb, come on," Archie said, surprising Rudy. "Show a little respect, would ya."

Sullen faced, Herb shook his head. "Nope."

He jumped in, wasting no time to back the vehicle out onto the street. The cab's absence left Rudy and Archie standing in the empty space looking at each other.

"Ever since he and Mr. Caesar's daughter shacked up, Herb thinks he can do what he wants," Archie said. "Just once, I'd like to give that pear-brain a good right to wake him up. . . . Okay, get out of here, Barabbas. I've got work to do. You're on again at 1:00 p.m. tomorrow. Don't be late."

With that attempt at a pleasant exchange and not looking for any reply, Archie made his way back to his office, leaving Rudy to find his way back to Kate's on foot.

***

Back on the streets, shadows played tricks with Rudy's mind, using his growing anxiety as volatile fuel. On his return trip to Kate's apartment, he expected one of their enemies to step out in front of him at any moment to finish what they started.

They're close by . . . I can feel it in me bones, he thought, rubbing folded arms against the cold as he walked along.

Where's that Dogg? She said she'd have me back.

He looked for her often, but she was never anywhere to be seen.

His instincts were serving him better than he knew, however. For, just minutes away from his position, a sinister meeting concerning him was taking place.

***

In a dusty cellar of an apartment building owned by Walter Kneebone, a corpse-gray, sullen-faced Vince Caracara sat on a simple chair at a small wooden table. Fist wrapped around a cruel switchblade, he dug into the top of the table aggressively with the tip.

The brim of his fedora was pulled down over his eyes, giving their shadowed profile a fiendish look. A single dusty lightbulb bathed the room in a dull yellow hue. Vince's neck bore a brutal scar from ear to ear. It was a memento of Insidio's work in both removal and reattachment of Vince's head back at the tannery. He also had a bloody .38 bullet hole in his right cheek and another two bloody bullet holes in the right shoulder of his suit jacket. On his chest three vicious knife wounds could be seen, highlighted by the blood marks on his white dress shirt worn to the meeting.

"Dead along with the rest is how it should have been," he said. He touched the weeping bullet hole in his cheek. "I never asked for this."

The memory of Insidio leering at him and then charging with his blood-soaked dagger in hand was burned into Vince's mind. There'd been the strangest silence and euphoric release after Insidio's first brutal and aggressive backhand slash. Three more inhuman bone-splintering stabs then struck his chest before he'd hit the floor lifeless. Then light—just the brightest light he'd ever known . . . uplifting, benevolent, it penetrated his entire being. Then came the terrifying fall, a plummet into that swirling black mass. He'd felt his velocity increase for what seemed like forever—well beyond the speed of sound. All the pain he'd ever caused another living soul saturated him in those moments. There were no words for that. It was just a paralyzing, endless scream of pain.

Then, suddenly, he became aware of being enveloped by an omnipotent force, and he heard a woman's voice. It was stern, unforgiving, hard. When he'd asked if she was God, all she did was laugh. It wasn't a joyful laugh. It was something mad, sinister beyond anything his own malicious personality could comprehend. If he'd had teeth then, they would have been gritted so tight as if to break. Her attention on him made him want to cower, terrified. She said he was lucky . . . lucky to be reborn and in *her* employ. She said he'd surrendered his free will and now belonged to her until his debt was paid. She ordered that he follow the instructions of Insidius to the letter. Failure to comply would result in immediate transmutation into the realm of hungry ghosts for eternity.

"Fuck you! Fuck all of you," Vince said at the table, grinding his teeth in indignation. "Bitch turned me into fucking Frankenstein."

Walter Kneebone stood at the bottom of the stairs on the edge of shadow, glaring at the resurrected criminal for a short time. "The cold in your bones is bad at first," he finally said. "Don't worry. You'll get used to it. It's because your blood ain't really pumping around your body anymore. 'Reanimation' they called it when I first woke up. And before you even think about runnin' and goin' off on some kill-everything revenge kick, there is no escape short of leaving the planet, which you can't do because you can't die until they say so, comprende? Believe me, I've tried it all. And I been at it for thirty-five years. There is *nowhere* they can't find you." He stepped forward into the light toward Vince. "And it hurts worse every time they do find you when you run. Just do what they want. Like I said, Vince, welcome to my world."

"This aint' livin'," Vince spat more than said.

"Look at the bright side: your head's back where it belongs. And you get a second chance to set things right and take revenge at the same time. Hey, we'd both like to get our hands on the spade, right?"

Vince dug the last letter of a name into the table, leaning hard on his six-inch switchblade: *BARABBAS.*

"Feels like you've been properly drowned and slapped back to life, doesn't it?" Walter said. "The scar doesn't look that bad. Looks like barbed wire, maybe a prison tattoo. Gives you street cred. At least he didn't gut you like he did me the first time. Said I should appreciate how my victims felt all at once. I got a scar looks like some bastard's dug a Grand Canyon from belly to my knee. When he caught me the last time, he stuck that friggin' dagger of his all the way through before pullin' down. Then he resurrected me just to show me he could do it so I could watch myself bleed to death a second time."

Vince replied by digging his knifepoint harder into the desk.

"You'll get over it, feller. Just do what they want and everything will be fixed right, ya get me?"

"They turned me into a freak-show, a fuckin' monster, Kneebone!"

"We were both monsters before our present situation, Vince, only I had better taste in clothes," said Walter.

That comment raised a curl of a smile on Vince's face.

"What we have to do is focus on the task they set us. I can't take getting cut to pieces another time for getting it wrong."

"So what do we do now, then?" Vince asked.

"We find where the spade is hiding. Once we hand him over to Insidius, they'll cut us some slack to do what we want till the next job. Your big advantage now is you pretty much can't be put down for good unless Insidius does it themselves."

Vince stood from the table and drove the knife into the center of the name, before looking up with a snarl at Walter Kneebone. "Let's go catch us a spade, then."

CHAPTER

8

Biting Shadows

Rudy made it back to Kate's apartment without incident. He now sat at the small kitchen table as she washed dishes, thinking about all that had taken place in last hours. A fork in his left hand hovered over the steak, potatoes, and beans Kate had provided soon after he'd arrived.

"You gonna' eat that?" she asked, looking at him over her shoulder. "It won't leap into your mouth by itself. . . . Hey! Earth to Rudy."

Rudy looked up at her. "Huh?"

"It's no good cold. Go on, dig in, then get some sleep before you fall over. Do you good to do something normal. Don't worry. No demon or badass serial killer's gonna find you here. Dogg spread a little of her magic around here. Keeps the boogeyman away—know what I mean?"

"I hope so," Rudy said. "Don't know how much more of it I can take."

He suddenly realized how tired and hungry he was, and demolished the meal in short order. Being terrified beyond speech while pursued by an Ultra Demon and their henchmen that ended in a gangland massacre *had* been hard work.

The meal done, Rudy soon found himself down a short hallway in a small but cozy bedroom. It was furnished with a single bed, a lamp next to an old, tan

TV chair in one corner, and a clothes wardrobe on another wall. Staring at the ceiling from the bed, hands behind his head, Rudy's mind flashed images like some badly cut B horror movie. Screams, sounds of bodies striking walls, menacing faces, and gunshots filled his audiovisual mindscape.

Where does it all go from here? Your life never gonna be the same, Rudy Barabbas. That's for sure.

He fell into an uneasy sleep for what the morrow would bring.

***

During REM sleep, if that's what it was, Rudy experienced being swept along through some kind of tangible black void. The chilling, sinister laugh of a woman, or was it some greater chaotic force, swirled around him as he was sucked into an unfathomable lightless pit. He finished with a bump on his backside onto a hard, dark surface. A spotlight overhead came on with a sharp snap-CLICK to highlight him in an otherwise endless black space. Then, surrounding him on all sides, preceded by a wave of intense foreboding, many billboard-sized faces of Insidia sped toward him. Each looked like some grand picture to be hung in an artist's gallery. Stopping some fifty feet away while still towering over him, each of her images smiled at him in her unsettling way.

"There you are. Now tell Momma where you're hiding so I can come get you," the face right in front of him said.

It all felt so real, as though he'd been sucked into another dimension.

"Come on, Golliwog. Cooperate and I'll be gentle," one face said.

"Where are you, Golliwog?" asked another.

"Let me help you," said yet another.

Rudy sat on the floor listening, eyes wide, mouth gaping, hands on the ground behind him as if he'd been pushed over. In the grip of abject fear, his throat felt constricted, incapable of response.

"DO AS YOU'RE TOLD . . . you sniveling ant," Insidia snapped. "Or I promise you, I'll shred the meat from your corpse and spread it on pizza for topping."

"Rudy . . . Rudy. Don't listen to her," came the soothing voice of Dogg. "They're trying to trick you into exposing your whereabouts. You're quite safe. Look to your left. In the distance there is a green door. Do you see it?"

Rudy's view swung left. There, under one of Insidia's pictures, bathed in a soft light was the green door.

"Got it!" Rudy said.

"Good. Now stand. Pay no attention to Insidia. She can't hurt you. That's it. Now move quickly to the door, turn the handle, and walk through."

"Golliwog, do as you are told and Insidia won't get cross. You won't like me at all when I'm cross. Just tell me where you are."

"Don't listen to her, Rudy. Come back to your bed. It's alright. That's it. A little farther, a little—"

Suddenly Rudy sat bolt upright in his bed, gasping for air while still horrified by his dream. Trying to sort reality from nightmare, his eyes darted about the dimly lit room.

"Over here, Rudy. It's alright. You're safe."

Startled, Rudy looked to his right to see Dogg sitting in the chair in the corner of the room.

"Well done," Dogg said. "A few more seconds and she would have known your location."

Rudy rubbed his face with both hands. "Oh God. What just happened?"

"Ultra Demons have the ability to dream-search a tethered subordinate."

"I thought you stopped that thing from working?"

"So did I. It was a well-hidden function that I missed. Sorry. They aren't called 'Insidius' for nothing, you know. It's dealt with now. They won't be able to use it to influence you again. Now get some rest. I'll watch over you. You have a big day ahead of you. Make sure you're at work on time tomorrow. I've heard the agents needing your help will be in the area very soon."

***

Morning came for Rudy like most any other with the ringing of an old alarm clock. He tried to pull the second pillow over his head to douse the sound, which failed miserably. Reaching blindly for the clock as he surfaced to consciousness to turn off the alarm, he smacked it, still clanging, to the floor instead. His eyes blinked open, with a deep frown to accompany it, and he rolled to reach for the clock again. Picking it up to shut the alarm off, he saw the hands pointing to eleven o'clock.

Wait a minute. A red, old-time alarm clock?

He swung his legs out of bed and pulled himself to a sitting position, holding the clock with both hands.

"This is me clock from me old flat across town. "

He shook his head, placing the clock back on the side table next to his bed. He noticed a familiar bag in the corner and another assortment of fresh-ironed, casual clothes in a stack on top of it. Then the smell of something pleasant being cooked down the hall caught his attention. After changing into clean clothes, Rudy slid his feet into his shoes and plodded out to see what might be on offer for breakfast.

He found Kate in the kitchen cooking up a storm while Dogg sat in one of three chairs to the left of the breakfast table.

"No, the rift to the Echaa Realms has been—Oh, Rudy, good morning," said Dogg, cutting the previous conversation short. "Sleep better the second time round?"

"Much, thanks. And what's the Echaa thing?" asked Rudy, taking a seat at the table on the right.

"Oh, nothing," Dogg said, "just some stale news Kate and I were talking about."

Kate turned away from the stove to pour a mug of coffee. Looking at Rudy, she set it down on the table. Rudy reached for the cup, and the first sip of coffee had him sigh as if a weight had been lifted of his shoulders.

"Very simple décor you had at your old place," Kate said. "Don't you like furniture? Had to check twice to see that somebody actually lived there until I found the mattress and the closet of clothes in the corner of the bedroom. Fridge in the kitchen didn't even show a memory of anything in it. Guess you eat out a lot."

"It was temporary," Rudy said drolly. "I was saving money until I found somewhere better for me and Mala, for when she comes to join me."

"Rudy, I'm afraid all that will have to go on hold for a time," Dogg said.

Rudy cut his eyes at Dogg. "What? No. Why?"

"Well, firstly we are unsure yet as to how things will unfold around you now. Secondly there is the jeopardy she would be placed in due to certain other interested parties wanting you under their control."

"You mean that black-hearted woman and her friends."

"If you can call them that," Dogg said. "And, yes, I do mean them. If your Mala were here, the first thing they would do is take her to get to you. They would do things to her—cruel and unspeakable things—until you complied."

"Oh . . . I didn't think of that," Rudy said. He set his coffee down and hung his head.

His eyes came up when Kate placed a large serving of pork belly, beans, and greens in front of him.

"Eat before you disappear," Kate said.

All Rudy's attention fell upon the hot plate of food in front of him. "Thanks, Kate. So good to have two solid meals in a row."

"Your life as you've known it is over, Rudy," Dogg said as Rudy dug into his breakfast. "Now listen. Today is likely to be one of mixed events. You'll need to keep your wits about you. I need you to be in the vicinity of the Frost Bank by 3:00 p.m."

"Frost Bank?"

"Yes, do you know where it is?"

"Of course. Why? What do I do there?"

"Just wait. We are in a fluid situation, Rudy. Insidius could return at any time. The allied agents I spoke of should be in that area in the next few hours. They'll need your help to find someone. You have the local knowledge they'll need, and they'll help protect you from those hunting you."

"But . . . I can't tell them—whoever they are—that I'm working for you, right?"

"Correct."

"You just want me to be driving around to bump into someone I have no description of? Then to help them find someone else whose face we have no description of either?"

"Well, yes."

Rudy sat up straight and placed the heel of his hand over one eye as if he had an ice cream headache.

"Don't worry, Rudy. Your karma will see the opportunity arise, I'm sure," Dogg said. "Soon my partner Uniss will likely join us too. He'll have updated information. Threads of all the lives involved are tied to you now."

"My karma? And who is Uniss?"

Dogg sighed. "Never mind. That's all I can say for now. Just know that, whilst we don't know exactly *what* will take place today, you are at the center of all that gravity."

Rudy frowned. "So I'm like the flypaper for all the flies to land on."

"Until we find who we are looking for, you're the best point of focus we've got."

"Wow," Rudy said almost under his breath.

"You'll be quite safe. I'll always have your back. Now it's time for you to finish up and get moving."

Rudy wolfed down the rest of his breakfast. Moments later he closed the door to the apartment behind him with a bump and headed back to begin his shift. He soon walked out onto the sidewalk and into a cold but dry day. Stepping off to catch the bus to work, his stomach began to churn, remembering that Walter Kneebone had booked his cab—all day. Maybe he should have mentioned that to Dogg, but . . . too late now.

He looked to the heavens for a moment. *Goddess, how will I get out of this one?*

CHAPTER

9

Who's who in this zoo

The cold didn't feel quite as bitter as the night before. Somehow the winter chill didn't penetrate through Rudy's clothing as it had always done. He brushed the front of his chest and thought about the new shirt they had given him.

What did she say, "perks of the job"?

That made him smile. Minutes later he caught the Number 11 bus on time —didn't even have to run to catch up like he normally would. On the bus, though, all he could think about was what he could do about avoiding picking up Walter Kneebone. He arrived at work with fifteen minutes to spare, just as Herb pulled up. Herb gave Rudy a sly smirk as he stepped out of the cab and tossed the keys to him, swinging the door shut with a thump behind him. Rudy's mouth fell open as he looked at the state of the cab they shared. Herb had somehow found a way for the cab to be less than the pristinely clean example Rudy had handed over the night before. The waft of air coming from the interior smelled distinctly of stale beer and cigarette smoke. Rudy waved a hand in front of his face to decrease the odor.

"Where have you been with, it mon? I can't take it out like that!"

"Oh, gee, so sorry," said Herb, tossing the ride a dismissive glance. "No time to run it through the wash. You handle it."

Rudy stood there staring at the filthy cab. He knew Archie would order it cleaned before he could go anywhere. That would eat into his shift and any bonus he might have earned.

Wait! Maybe I can use this to get out of dealing with Walter Kneebone.

With Herb standing there leering at him like he'd won some cheap point in an argument, Rudy stepped past him and sat in the driver's seat.

"Take your time at the wash bay, kid," Herb said, beginning to laugh.

Rudy surveyed the mess and looked back at Herb. With a sour expression Rudy slammed the door. As the door thumped shut, every bit of dirt, grunge, and odor fell away, vaporizing. It was like someone had tapped it with a magic wand. Herb's mouth fell open so wide upon seeing it happen that he could have started his own wind tunnel mouthing the words, *What the fuck?*

Rudy couldn't believe what had just happened either, but he liked it—a lot. Then he looked in his side mirror. Behind him, sitting in the shadowy far corner of the depot, he saw Dogg watching him. Her sapphire-blue eyes seemed to be glowing. He could have sworn she was smiling too, if that was possible for a canine. Rudy looked back to Herb, still standing there dumbstruck. Rudy flashed a wide, toothy grin, then flipped Herb the finger as he reached for the gearshift.

"Hey, Barabbas!" Archie called from his office door. "You're to pick up Mr. Kneebone at the Frost Bank at 2:30. Wait for him 'til he shows."

Rudy breathed a sigh of relief that he didn't have to get Walter right away, also noting that it was the location where Dogg said she wanted him. Then, to make it sound like he was disappointed, he asked Archie, "What happened to 'the whole shift'?"

"What am I, your weather girl?" Archie said. "He says he wants you there at 2:30, then it's 2:30. Just be on time, got it?"

Sliding the cab into drive, Rudy pressed the gas pedal and rolled out of the bay to begin his shift, on time.

***

The first hour or so of his shift was pretty mundane. He had a few short-run fares and a no-show. He couldn't help but be suspicious of everyone who got in his cab that day, even the little old lady with her shopping bags. Any minute he expected one of the bad guys to be standing in front of his cab. Then, about an hour and a half into his shift, a neatly dressed young man wearing a brown fedora flagged him down on a street corner.

"Hemisfair Arena," the passenger said in an out-of-town accent.

Another of those Oklahoma dudes. Hmm, had a couple of those last week. Rudy paused his thoughts and then mused, *Hemisfair Arena? Hm, must be some convention in town.*

Rudy pointed the cab in the direction of San Antonio's premiere basketball venue and drove on. With the weather more tolerable today, more people were out on the streets. Traffic flow was slow in places. Rudy had the radio on softly, with some Motown tunes filling the background. He kept a subtle check on the guy in the backseat for any signs of danger. Even made an attempt at small talk with the guy, who kept looking out the passenger window while grunting one-word answers.

Conversation dropped off about the time they passed the Frost Bank, one of the oldest banks in the city. Dogg's earlier instructions rang in his mind, as did Archie's orders to pick up Kneebone there in a little while. As they drove past the bank, Rudy paid particular attention to see if anything stood out. Nothing. Then his blood froze for a moment when he thought he saw Walter Kneebone going through the main doors at the top of the steps. But he lost sight of whoever it was as the direction and topography cut off his view. It didn't take long after that before they were making their way toward the Hemisfair Arena fan's entrance. Being the middle of the day, the parking lot was mostly empty, and Rudy only noticed a few people about. The cab rolled along parallel to some older buildings at 10 miles an hour.

With about a hundred yards to go, the guy in the back spoke up. "Stop here."

Rudy complied and pulled up to the curb in line with an alleyway separating two of the buildings.

"Wait here," the guy said and got out.

He walked past the front of the vehicle with Rudy eyeing him. The guy was about thirty feet away when he looked over his shoulder at Rudy and seemed to smile. At that moment the back door on the driver's side swung open and someone entered the cab.

"Hello, spade."

Even as he felt his heart clench, Rudy's eyes darted to the rearview mirror. There, within arm's length and glaring at him with lifeless, cold yellow eyes was the murderous face of Vince Caracara. His fedora's brim was pulled down to his eyes and gave his gray cadaverous features a sinister look. The bullet that had punctured his face had become a blotch-knitted scar.

Rudy swallowed, noting vaguely that Vince's brown fedora matched the hat of the fare he'd just dropped off.

"Don't look so surprised, boy. You knew we'd come for ya." Vince's expression turned to a wicked sneer. "Now you're gonna—"

Rudy dove across the seat for the front passenger door and yanked down on the handle.

"Hey, c'mere!" Vince shouted. At the same time, he reached forward and grabbed at Rudy.

"Ahhh!" Rudy screamed.

He felt his heart beating so hard that he figured Vince could hear it.

Goddess . . . Dogg . . . someone help me!

***

Vince tried to hold Rudy with one hand; the other gripping the cruel blade he always carried to kill or coerce. But Rudy shoved the door open and scrambled out on his hands and knees as Vince continued to grasp for him.

"Come here!" Vince snarled through gritted teeth, now lunging toward the rear passenger door.

He threw it wide open to climb out as Rudy scrambled to his feet. Facing the alley, Rudy gathered his legs under him and, looking straight ahead, bolted for all he was worth into the shadow-filled passage.

"Come out, spade," Vince called, walking forward. "There's nowhere to run. I'd prefer you in one piece, but several will do if I have to. They can stick you back together later."

Vince stopped a few steps inside the alley, waiting. He knew Rudy had run into a dead end. No answer or movement came after a long awkward silence. Then Vince heard a small shuffle and something fall with a clatter to ground.

"Get your ass out here, boy!" Vince yelled. "I've got you like a rat in a box. . . . Fine, then. You won't come out like a man, I'm comin' in there to cut an ear off just for makin' me walk."

His face hot with anger, Vince headed into the alley, looking for his pound of flesh.

***

Deep inside the alley, light was pretty poor, even for mid-afternoon. Several Dumpsters stood adjacent to a rear-building exit. Rudy crouched beside a Dumpster and some garbage cans after finding every back door locked from the inside and nowhere else to run. Terrified of losing his life, he quietly picked up the garbage can lid he'd knocked over moments earlier to mount some sort of defense. Soft footsteps approached. Fear grew inside Rudy like a hungry beast eating a hole in his gut the size of a cathedral.

A way out! Need a way out!

He looked up. The break in the roofline of the buildings above seemed to close in on him. It felt like he'd run into a prison cell. He hoped for some intervention from Dogg . . . somebody . . . anybody.

Where are you, Dogg? his mind screamed.

The footsteps drew closer—close enough that Rudy could hear the gritty crunch under the soles of Vince's shoes. Then the footsteps stopped. Now Vince was within easy arm's reach.

"I'm gonna cut you bad, spade. I'll cut you less if you show yourself. Time to pay the man."

Rudy stayed there, crouched, looking toward Vince, whose silhouette was now plain to see. Rudy watched a blue light suddenly skitter across the surface of the ground from his right. As the wave of light rolled under the soles of his shoes, for a moment his feet felt magnetized, drawn to the ground, throwing him off balance. Then, just as suddenly, the force holding his shoes broke and he toppled backward. The rippling blue light swept past Vince, dissipating as it broke against the wall opposite.

"I see you there, spade," Vince said.

"I see you too, Vincent Luka Caracara," came Dogg's voice from the darkness opposite. "You've been a very bad boy."

"Who's that?" asked Vince, brandishing his knife. "Come out here. Come see what I've got for you."

From out of the shadows padded Dogg, which prompted Rudy to stand.

"You were here all the time?" Rudy asked.

"Long enough," Dogg said, staying back out of Vince's sight.

"Who is that?" Vince shouted. "Show yourself!"

Vince looked to Rudy and then past Dogg for the person belonging to the voice. He attempted to move in Dogg's direction and found both feet anchored to the ground.

"Hey! What is this?" Vince shouted.

Furious, he wrenched his right leg forward, managing to drag barely half a step before the ground itself enveloped his shoes, fixing him in place.

"What the fuck!" Vince looked down at his feet. "Come out of there, you fuckin' rat." He slung a scowl at Rudy. "You! Stay put. I'll deal with you in a minute."

Rudy looked at Dogg, unsure of what to do.

"Time for you to go, Rudy. Mr. Caracara and I need to have a little chat. Just give him a wide berth if you don't mind. You'll have to deal with the individual at the entrance, though. I'm afraid immobilizing Mr. Caracara will take all of my attention."

Vince tried with all his strength to step toward Rudy, but remained rooted to the ground. "Goddamn it! What is this?"

Enraged, he threw his blade at Rudy's chest. The blade sped across the space, skewering the garbage can lid Rudy barely managed to raise in time. He looked down to see five inches of the blade protruding through the sheet metal. The tip had nicked his jacket, leaving a nail-sized puncture.

"Go, Rudy!" Dogg said. "It's nearly time."

Careful to stay out of Vince's reach, Rudy held onto the lid with the knife still stuck in it, covering his chest. Vince lunged at him a couple times but only managed to take skin off his knuckles on the lid. Rudy made a break for it and got past Vince.

"Come back here, you fuckin' rat! I'm gonna . . . I'm gonna . . ."

Ignoring Vince's rage, Rudy ran, heading for his cab. From behind he heard a horrendous crash, as if every garbage can and dumpster in the alley had been picked up and dropped on the screaming gangster.

Rudy now saw the other guy in the fedora standing between him and his one chance of escape. He charged at him like a madman and swung the garbage lid wildly at the thug's face. The swing cleaned the guy's clock, knocking him sprawling to the ground. When the guy tried to get to his feet, Rudy held the lid with both hands and gave him another solid belt across the head for good measure.

"You like that? Have another!" He swung his improvised shield yet again.

CLANG!

"Stay down!" Rudy shouted.

He climbed into the cab, dropping the lid onto the seat beside him, Vince's knife still embedded as a trophy.

Then Rudy sped away, headed for Frost Bank—and to search for Dogg's mysterious friends.

Not quite

THE END

<<<<>>>

About the Author

Yuan Jur served in the Australian military as a young adult. He later sought the solitude of monastic life serving the community as an ordained Buddhist monk for many years. In Buddhism's warrior-caste arm known in the West as Zen he achieved the rank of abbot and theologian. As a theologian, Yuan Jur studied many belief systems, doctrines and ideologies from around the world. During those decades he also gained a master's degree in Chinese martial arts and medieval weaponry.

In 2007 a life threatening illness ended his monastic career and nearly his life. During recovery, Yuan Jur turned to a new venture. He combined his knowledge gained from decades of belief systems study with a love of Time Travel Paranormal alt/world fantasy as a young man. The result was a totally new immersive superverse series called Citadel 7. By 2014 his first Citadel 7 series combined trilogy had won both blue ribbon and Grand Prize in the Chanticleer Cygnus international writing Awards. He states: "There is a lot, lot more to come."